Dade &. SaeKu. Two
A Bronx Tale

The Prologue...

As the water was poured over Pryce's head, her arms began to flap and cries belted from her lungs. She gasped for air, as if the was drowning, trying her best to grab ahold of her mother's arms –as if she'd ever let her go.

"Aight, nigga. That's enough." Lorde reached over and grabbed the small cup from the pastor's hand, and his other hand at his chest. "You're going to need more than God if you drown her." he whispered.

"LORDE!" Sage chastised, straightening him up with just one word.

"Aight. Aight." He handed the pastor the cup, and stepped back a bit.

A slight snicker left SaeKu's lips, but she quickly pulled her herself together as she felt a demonic set of eyes staring a hole into the side of her heads.

Turning sideways, she caught wind of the angry set of eyes that rested upon her gentle skin. Suddenly, her cheeks became flushed and her nerves were deemed rattled. Without another sound, she cut away, facing the ground. Feeling a lot less than, SaeKu refused to return the nasty glared. Instead, she lifted her head once more and allowed herself to feel sorry just for a minute.

It would take much more than a miracle to reduce the amount of hatred in the heart of the man that she loved with each fiber of her being. The hollow void that not being with or around him formed within SaeKu had broken her spirit and claimed her happiness. But she'd done the unforgivable. She'd went against everything that they stood for, and all that they'd been through. She'd saw fit to curse his name, and bring him the worst pain known to man. Her acts were unforgivable, and there was no way around the fact.

As the preacher continued with the sermon, hand claps sounded throughout the church, pulling SaeKu from her trance. A smile appeared across her lips as Sage turned to her beaming with pride. Simultaneously, they'd both joined church with the intentions of gaining a closer relationship with God.

Sage wanted to understand forgiveness and offer it to herself, being that she'd never quite forgave herself for being so upset with her parents. She'd blamed herself for their death since the day that it had happened. On the other hand, SaeKu was begging for God's forgiveness, instead. She understood that she was broken, and in need of a good fixing.

After service, the sun beamed as everyone stepped whisky winds that nature had offered during the cold December month.

"Our house, right?" Sage turned to SaeKu and tugged at her coat.

"Yes. Of course."

"Don't take all day SaeKu. Pryce will notice if her teetee is missing."

"Tell your mother to put a little faith in me." SaeKu grabbed Pryce's chubby cheeks and shook them. "I'm going to be right behind you guys."

"Good." Sage drew closer to her best friend. "Are you okay."

"Yeah." SaeKu nodded.

"I mean, really." Sage questioned. "Are you okay?"

"I'll be fine, Sage."

"Sorry that he…"

"There's no need to be sorry. Dade is going to be Dade. Maybe one day this will all blow over and that man can stop hating my guts."

"Yeah. Maybe one day." Sage nodded. "See you in a few."

Sage continued down the steps, leaving SaeKu to her lonesome. As she watched Dade and Lorde embrace, thoughts of reaching out crossed her mind. Guessing he could feel her eyes focused on his frame, Dade looked up towards the church. There wasn't an ounce of sympathy or sign of recant as he locked eyes with the sinking soul that he'd lost all hope for. Unlike the time before, and many others, SaeKu held her ground, not looking away. She was tired of feeling sorry for herself, and mourning the lost of a love that was destined.

"Oh well." SaeKu shrugged, gathering her bearings and moving towards her vehicle. She'd recently upgraded to a Lexus SUV, and was head over heels in love with her new whip.

**

"Sage, you put too much fucking seasoning on these green beans. Fuck you trying to do? Take a nigga out before his time." Lorde barked, spitting his greens on the plate.

"Lorde, they're not even bad."

"Bad? Them motherfuckers are horrible. That's why you didn't even put none on your plate. Them cooking shows ain't helping, baby. I appreciate the effort, but this is the last time you're cooking for me."

"Why are you always so fucking aggravating?" Sage asked with her hands in the air.

"I'm just saying. It's all good, but a nigga hiring a personal chef to teach you how to cook. That's the only thing stopping a nigga from marrying your ass, for real."

"Lorde, I'm the only thing stopping you from marrying me. You won't fix your mouth to ask, because you fuck up so much that you're afraid I'm going to say no."

"Why you always bringing up the past? Damn." Lorde had gotten caught up in a few sticky situations.

Never had he gotten caught cheating or disrespecting Sage, but there were instances with other females that she didn't approve of. When they first made things official, it wasn't as easy as Lorde had thought. The commitment thing was a little much for him, so he attempted to keep his hoes on the low. That didn't work very well, because Sage was on his ass like white on rice.

Needless to say, she threatened to end them if he didn't clean out his contacts and retire his old cell number. Unlike anyone else in life, besides Lauren, Lorde abided by her rules. Within 3 hours of her mentioning leaving him alone, again, he had switched up the entire game on his old hoes.

"Hmmm." Sage shrugged, not giving a fuck. Lorde's ways were beginning to rub off on her. She'd been forced to grow tougher skin due to his harshness and unpredictable outburst.

"I can't wait until tonight." Lorde hissed.

"Why is that Lorde?"

"Because I'm going to have your smart mouth ass backing up every fucking word that just fell from them big ass lips of yours. Watch. When I put this dick on you, I bet you won't have all of that shit to say."

"I'll be back talking in about…" Sage check the Rolex on her arm, and turned her lips up. "Five minutes. That's about all you need, right?"

Sage's statement drew laughter from the table's participants, at Lorde's expense. SaeKu forked her spaghetti, having not much of an appetite. The cramps that she were feeling had her not wanting to do much of anything.

Dade looked on with concern etched across the lining of his forehead. He noticed SaeKu hadn't touched anything on her plate. Although it took everything out of him to acknowledge it, he did, anyhow.

"You're just going to sit there and starve." He probed, not even giving her the satisfaction of eye contact. "Hm?"

"Excuse me." SaeKu slid back from the table, threw her napkin beside her plate, and stood. "I need to use the bathroom."

Swiftly, SaeKu turned in the direction of the bathroom. Once inside of the bathroom, she let out a huge gush of wind. Just hearing him acknowledge her after so long was breathtaking. In that moment, she craved everything that they once shared.

Another cramp soared through her body, causing her to seat herself on the toilet. After pulling her underwear down, she searched for blood but there was no sign. Sighing, she stood, not ready for that time to come.

"Thank God." SaeKu got up and turned on the water to wipe herself up.

Stepping from the bathroom, she was startled by Dade's presence. He was standing in the hallway, along side of the bathroom. He'd thickened over the months, using the gym to burn off the frustrations he felt within. His caramel complexion sent electric waves through SaeKu's spine. The hairs on the back of her neck stood at attention at the sound of his voice.

"I think it's about time that we talked. Wouldn't you agree?" Dade grilled.

SaeKu searched for an answer, but couldn't find one. Her head dropped to the ground, and then back up at Dade. Both of their eyes were big as saucers when SaeKu stated the obvious.

"I think my water just broke." She confirmed the gush of water that was flowing from between her legs. Back down at the floor and, then, up towards Dade, SaeKu's head continued to move.

Dade &. SaeKu. Two
A Bronx Tale

Chapter

6 months later…

    SaeKu was pulled from her thoughts at the sound of the captain's voice, alerting everyone that the plane had landed. Shuffling was heard amongst the passengers as she stood at the head of the plane, waiting for the door to open. Her smile was big and bright as she directed passengers to the exit gateway and thanked them for flying with American Airlines.

    As the last passenger exited the plane, SaeKu peeped at the back of the plane to be sure that Sage was handling the cleanup. It was go time, and having to stay behind and clean the cabin wasn't in either of their plans. With a thumbs up, Sage confirmed that everything was good on her end.

After an hour, both SaeKu and Sage were treading through the airport with one destination in mind. Their next flight wasn't for another four hours, so they had time to blow. Reaching into her pocket, SaeKu checked the time, noting that she had a few minutes to spare before her daughter's evening nap. Putting pep into her step, she sped up to decrease the time it would require for her to make it to her room and check in.

Fortunately, SaeKu was sticking the key card into the hotel room door less than fifteen minutes after stepping off the plane. Hotels that were affiliated with the airport were preferable, so she'd struck gold. Placing her bags at the door, she fell over onto the bed, and dialed the seven digits that she remembered better than the spelling of her first name. On the second ring, she received an answer.

"Where's my baby, Dade?" SaeKu questioned before he could acknowledge her call.

"Right here, where else would she be?" he huffed. "Answer."

Pulling the phone from her face, SaeKu waited for the FaceTime to connect after accepting. It was the same routine, more often than not. If SaeKu didn't know any better, it was for Dade's benefit rather than their daughter. If she wasn't attempting to eat the phone, then she didn't want anything to do with it.

"HEY MAMAS!" SaeKu beamed as her daughter's face appeared on her screen. "Dido!" she called her name, hoping to win her attention. That did the trick, as usual.

Dido's chocolate skin maneuvered and a near toothless smile appeared on her face. "Hey baby girl." SaeKu began to hype her little spirit. Slob poured from her chubby cheeks and small laughter emitted from her body. "Hey. Hey. Hey Dido." SaeKu continued hyping her baby girl.

"Alright, it's time for me to put her down for a nap." Dade turned the camera towards him, and warned. "Where you at?"

"In a city. On the clock." SaeKu sassed.

"And where's that?" Dade didn't give a fuck that she didn't want to tell him her whereabouts. It was the same thing every time she left.

"Atlanta Dade." She sighed, rolling her eyes into the ceiling.

"You can roll them bitches into the ground for all I give a fuck. I'm just trying to know where the fuck my daughter's mother is when she's not with her. Nothing more. Nothing less, B." Dade shrugged. Without another word, he disconnected the call.

He had managed to find ways to step on SaeKu's nerves even on the calmest days. Unfortunately for her, he was somewhat the baby daddy from hell. It was baffling as to why he was fond of hassling her, but barely even mentioned the mother of his other daughter. If SaeKu had to guess, he was still being an asshole about the entire abortion fiasco, but it had been over a year. Their daughter was alive and kicking him, giving him no reason to continue to spew hatred towards her.

It didn't make things any better that he insisted that Dido spend her work days at his home, and not in the care of a nanny or sitter. He'd set so many rules for her care that SaeKu often questioned if she'd even took part in carrying and birthing her.

**

The beating at SaeKu's door startled her, pulling her from her deep slumber. She'd cried herself to sleep, hoping to wake up from the miserable nightmare that she'd been sucked into. Once her ears adjusted to the sound, she was well aware of who was knocking at her door as if they were the fire marshal attempting to get inside.

Dragging herself from the coach, which she'd been too drained to move from, SaeKu slowly walked towards the door. Stepping on her tippy toes to be sure of the visitor, SaeKu checked her peephole. Surely, Dade was standing on the other side of the door. He was raising his hand to knock again, but she pulled the door open before he could.

"How…" he begin, pushing his way into the apartment. "I considered you to be a lot of things when you walked out of my life, but none of them of which were anything in comparison to what this fucking message is saying you are." He started. His curls were untamed and unkempt. Worry lines crossed his forehead as he searched SaeKu's body language for a sign of regret. He witnessed nothing of the such. "And to blame me for you sick twisted ass decision."

"You said that having a child was too much work, and…"

"And that if it wasn't with you, then I wasn't having another one. I know what I said. I may not have said that, but that's what I meant. Do you know what this has done? Do you know what you have done?" Dade questioned.

"Dade, I."

"Don't fucking Dade me. Don't you think that I should've had some type of say before you went to the chop shop and butchered my fucking child, SaeKu? Our child? Did you at least think about how much I would've wanted this, or were you too fucking selfish and bent on Daicee's unexpected appearance in my life? Huh? How the fuck can an innocent child's existence drive you up the roof that much to make you kill your own because of her? Huh? Let me ask you… What the fuck did she ever do to you?"

"That wasn't the…"

"Answer me, dammit!" Dade yelled, veins popping out the side of his neck.

"If this is some sick twisted get back shit that you are on, then I pray you burn in hell!" Dade mustered up the strength to say.

"I did not deserve that." Tears caused his eyes to swell. "You did

not deserve that." He didn't have the energy to turn back after

hearing SaeKu continue to call his name. Pleading her case would

get her nowhere. She was dead in his book. Finished.

SaeKu remembered the day as if it was yesterday. She

wished that he'd given her the chance to tell him the she had not

been able to go through with the procedure, but he'd stormed out just

as fast as he'd come inside. It would be four months before their

eyes would meet, again. In that moment, he realized that she'd been

true to her character, and never aborted their child. However, he

couldn't bring himself to mumble a word to her. That was the start of

their spiraling parenthood.

With the cream sickle body wash, SaeKu rubbed the back of

her thighs and then the dip that connected them with the lower half

of her legs. The fresh vanilla scent filled her nostrils, relaxing her

beyond belief. A deep sigh emitted from her throat, reminding her of

how drained she was from the day's events.

Quickly, her thoughts traced back to her child's father, wondering where his head was the majority of the time, and why he was intending for her to live a miserable life. SaeKu had never known Dade to be bitter and so dysfunctional. However, the birth of their daughter and uncanny situation had turned him ice cold.

Shrugging, she figured that the best she could do for their situation was to continue to pray. God had been working with her, continuously, and she prayed that Dade found the same fate. His pride had turned him into the ugliest monster with the meanest attitude. While SaeKu couldn't take the harshness in the beginning, she'd become accustomed to his tongue lashing over time.

Continuing to cleanse her body and soul, she tried to relocate memories of the two that consisted of more tasteful dialogue and behavior. Dade was once her knight in shining armor. She'd nearly killed for the man, and had never regretted the act. Now, they were living within the walls of one another's world and couldn't stand the sight of each other. More so on Dade's end, because SaeKu simply wanted to make peace.

The constant back and forth was redundantly imprudent. If SaeKu could have it her way, then co-parenting would be much more of a breeze. This rough dynamic that Dade considered functional was merely even structured in the least bit. Something would have to give, and soon.

SaeKu paused, now near her toes. It occurred to her. *Maybe he still has interest after all, and is timid about the decision to come forth.* SaeKu pondered, wondering if Dade was still contemplating them, coupled and happy. *Na.* She quickly tossed the insane assumption out of the shower.

SO, what could it possibly be? She lifted her head after cleansing her lower half. Evenly distributing soap over her subtle breast, SaeKu became frustrated with the unknown. For once, in a very long time, she wanted to know what was so damn difficult about Dade making amends. Again, she paused. This time, she nodded, thinking more wisely.

He's still hurting. The thought was more convincing than the first, so she went with it. "He's still hurting." SaeKu mouthed. She was trying to convince herself that it was the backing of Dade's actions towards her. It was his excuse. It was his reasoning.

Standing under the shower head to rinse herself, she closed her eyes and fell deep into oblivion. SaeKu, quickly, placed Dade on the backburner. She knew that if there wasn't anything in the world worse than a scorn woman, a scorn man would take the ladder. They were the worse kind.

**

Applying pressure, squeezing the phone between his fingers, Dade refrained from dialing SaeKu back. He battled the same feelings each day, knowing that one day he'd have to give in to them. Worry lines were etched across her chocolate skin, causing Dade to want to reach out and touch her. The contortion of her beautiful face at his forceful projection made Dade's dick stand. She brushed him off, effortlessly, each time he struck. Maturity was so fucking sexy on her.

"Come on, Dido. Let's get you down for a nap. Daicee went out without a fight. Let's see how long you can last."

Dade chuckled to himself, knowing that Dido would give him difficulty. Just like her mother, she was causing more gray strands of hair to appear on his noggin and goatee. His little woman was full of it, and everyone knew it.

She was every ounce of her old lady. Dade found himself running tired and raggedy behind her, just as he had SaeKu for so many years. And just like her old lady, her features were the most exotic and alluring. Dade would get lost in her sometimes, not wanting to be pulled from the trance that he was captured in.

Deep into her nursery, Dade removed the pre-made bottle of breast milk and placed it in the warmer that was plugged in whenever she visited. As he waited for the milk to heat, his thoughts found SaeKu again. It amazed him how she was able to even get a minute to suck the healthy fluid from her enlarged breast to supply enough for their daughter in her absence. In Dade's eyes, she was superwoman, but he would never tell her that he thought so. It was the main reason that he took their daughter off of her hands as often as he possibly could.

Taking a seat in the "manly" chair made for rocking, Dade cradled his daughter in his arms, pushing her further into his chest after a second. Looking down at her blemish-free skin, she reminded him of the possibilities of what could've been. It wasn't that he loved either of his daughters more than the other, but there was something about Dido that did it for him.

Dade had every reason to believe that it was due to the fact that he was insanely in love with the woman that birthed her, and could never truly experience his desires and fantasies with her. The love that he shared for her mother, but couldn't reveal, was poured into the makings of them both.

The whistling of the warmer alerted Dade, pulling him from a far away space –one where his head often roamed. Her bottle was ready. Lifting himself with Dido still in his arms, he made his way back to the other side of the room. Grabbing the bottle, he swung it back and forth to shake the access water that was dangling onto the plastic.

After a minute or so, he brought the bottle closer. Dade tested the milk on his hand before stuffing the powder pink nipple into his daughter's mouth. Of course, their chunky little being was receptive of the naturally curated liquid. It was her favorite pastime, sipping until she faded away. They'd ordered the special kind, one's that were to mimic the shape of a mother's breast in order for Dido to find comfort even when she couldn't nurse. In knowing that SaeKu would be up in the air, they were prone to comfort keepers, and the expensive ass bottles were some of them.

"Now, settle down big legs. It's naptime." Dade rocked back and forth, chin pointed towards the air.

As he continued to rock his daughter to the slow and steady beat that he'd conformed in his head, he found himself drifting as well. Not only had Dido gone down without a fight, but he was right behind her. Both sat in the depth of the nursery, resting their bones.

Chapter Two

"Arch that fucking back!" Lorde howled.

Obeying, Kassie leaned forward even more and backed her ass up into the air to match his height. The room was silent, other than the sound of Lorde pounding into the thickness of her bottom.

"Ew. Ewwww. Ewwww." Kassie responded to his vicious strokes. Although there had not been many, Lorde was the best partner that she'd ever joined in bed. Her natural tresses hung wildly down her back, lifting each time his thighs made contact with the back of hers.

"Where you going?" Lorde questioned, pulling Kassie backwards. She was damn near at the headboard while he stood on the floor chasing behind her. "Be still!" he commanded. "Be still."

He slowed his pace, seeing as though Kassie was having a difficult time handling the bulk that he had to offer. Her petite frame was no match for his large stature.

"Ewwwww. Ew. Ewwww. Shit." Kassie's cream coated the rubber that was slipping and sliding, helping Lorde to maneuver with ease.

"Play with it." Lorde replied with a low grumble.

"No. Unh. Unh."

Kassie refused, knowing that their session would end abruptly if she tickled her kitty. She had the weirdest reaction to clitoral stimulation. Her walls would entrap her victim, barely giving him room to continue stroking. Her shit would swell, puffy enough to give the illusion of fresh virgin pussy. Without a doubt, Lorde would be busting, and Kassie simply wasn't ready.

It wasn't because she wanted to prolong their sexual session, but it was because she wanted to prolong his visit. She'd damn neared had to suck his dick through his jeans just to get him to stay a little while longer. Needless to say, it's how she ended up bent over her bed with his jeans gathered around his legs.

"Do it."

"Lorrrrrrrrrrde." Kassie screamed. "Oh my Go…. Ummmmm." Lorde was stroking her with patience and passion. Her ass continued to press against his hips and thighs, causing a unique sensation to shoot from his toes. He knew that his time was coming, and wanted Kassie to get her rocks off again.

Leaning forward, he reached around and found her clit, himself. She squirmed when he made contact, flickering his finger back and forth.

"Cum for daddy. Cum on this dick." He encouraged.

"Oh. Shit. Oh shit. Ewwwwwww! Shit." Kassie closed her eyes and bit her bottom lip. Her face turned beet red as she began to ride the wave that Lorde had sent her on. Her body shuttered, weakening as something within her lifted her high above her own body.

"AWHHHH!" she screamed. "I'm cummmmmmmmmming."

Just as he'd anticipated, Kassie's pussy tightened around his shaft, pulling the nut that he'd been holding back out of the tip of his dick. His cum filled the XXL condom as his eyes rolled into the back of his head.

Falling over onto the bed, he slapped Kassie on the ass. It was only the third or fourth time that he'd hit the pussy, and it seemed to get better with time. He was learning more about her body, and that shit was on point.

Kassie had started out as a revenge fuck, a piece of a puzzle, a part of a plot, but she was quickly becoming Lorde's little jump off. He'd coded her name in his cell, and gave her a bit more time than he should have on the daily. Each time that he left her loft, he felt as guilty as a murderer on trial for life.

If his woman ever found out about the shit he was into during his spare time, all hell would break lose. That was exactly why he rarely saw Kassie for over an hour. It was his limit, and she was well aware of it. Tonight, he'd failed miserably at restricting her advances to go over their limit.

Lorde laid for a few before lifting to wash himself of Kassie's remains. Although he couldn't bathe, and seem suspicious, he wiped himself down well. The hot towel was refreshing as Lorde wiped away the evidence of infidelity. He cursed himself, standing in the bathroom alone, trying to wrap his head around what the fuck he was doing. He had the best of the best at home, and he was out on some foolish shit.

Tossing the towel on the sink, Lorde walked out of the bathroom looking as he had when he walked through the door of her place. "I'm out." He stated, but didn't receive a response. As usual, Kassie was dead to the world. She wouldn't be waking until the next morning for sure.

**

"Hey." Sage beamed, happy that her man was finally home.

"Hey."

There was nothing cheerful about Lorde's demeanor, causing Sage to sadden all of a sudden. She hated when his street life spilled over into their night, because it lessened their time together. Whenever Lorde was in a shitty mode, sleep was soon to follow his arrival.

Lorde refused eye contact as he stalked to the bathroom. Behind him, he closed the door before locking it. Lorde emptied his bladder while pulling his shirt from his head, and tossing it into the dirty clothing bend.

"Shit." He cursed, shaking before flushing the toilet.

With the quickness, Lorde removed the shirt he'd just tossed into the bend and placed it at his nose. Thankfully, Kassie's sent was not in tow. Sighing, Lorde tossed the shirt back into the hamper, and did the same with his pants and boxers after.

Sighing, Sage fell back against the plush headboard and went into deep thought. As of lately, there had been something up with Lorde that she couldn't quite pinpoint. If her intuition counted for anything, she would say that he was stepping out on her, but she didn't want to make assumptions.

Blowing out fresh air, she placed thoughts of Lorde on the backburner, and called SaeKu. She wanted to be sure that their plans to travel to Philly were in tact. The children would be taking the ride with them, and they needed to solidify all details concerning them.

"Hey. What's up?" Sage spoke.

"Nothing. Just landed. I'm glad that you called. Listen, Bella texted earlier and insisted that we come a bit earlier to get the girls settled and get some girl time in before the big party. I'm down for it, but I wanted to make sure that you were cool with it as well."

SaeKu was immune to the hustle and bustle of the busy airways. She strolled through, effortlessly, with her suitcase in tow. The uniform that she wore, religiously, tugged at her rounded hips and thick thighs. She hadn't even noticed the pair of eyes that she'd summoned with the way that her ass fell victim to the dramatics as she switched, passing terminal after terminal.

"Yeah. That's completely fine. I could use the free time. I promise." Sage huffed, hearing the shower running reminded her of her faint reality. She was clueless as to what was up with her man, but she was sure that things would either blow up or blow over. Either way, a girls trip to get it off of her mind sounded like a fantastic idea.

"Great. I'll let her know. Let me get off of this phone, and go to get this child of mine. I miss her little cheeks." SaeKu cooed.

"Alright. I'll talk to you later."

"Okay."

SaeKu ended the call, and slowed to read a text that had just came through from Dade.

"Excuse me." she heard from behind. Turning around, 180 degrees, SaeKu looked up to find a long legged, handsome, dark toned, rough neck peering down at her small frame. She wasn't the shortest, but this awfully delectable stature made her feel minute.

"Yes?" SaeKu questioned with a raise of the brown.

She trailed his legs up to his slender frame. When he begin to speak, a smile tugged at his cheeks, causing his left dimple to appear. Although uninterested, SaeKu was appreciative of his figure and features.

"I was wondering if you were coming on or getting off? … Work." He added, being sure to give clarity in addition to his question.

"Off actually, thank God."

"Perfect. I know it's not much, but you seem like a pretty busy young woman and I wanted to borrow a minute of your time. It's a bar just around…"

"That corner, and then hang a right. Yeah." SaeKu finished his statement.

Still smiling, he nodded. "I'm assuming you get this shit all the time." he looped his hands through the straps of the backpack he sported.

"No, but with this demanding ass job, sometimes I invite myself for a sit down." SaeKu admitted.

"Well, this time, I'm inviting you. You got somewhere you trying to be, or can you spare thirty minutes."

SaeKu wanted to decline, but she figured what the hell. At least he hadn't asked for her number, because that would've surely gotten him a no.

"Come on, now. We waiting right here, when we could've be done hit that corner." The young man pointed. "And hung a right."

He gaged a laugh from SaeKu as he attempted to mimic her from just a few seconds prior. "Okay. Okay." SaeKu chuckled.

"Girl, 'm glad you didn't turn me down. I didn't have shit else to come at you with. I would've jumped on that plane mad as fuck."

"I didn't catch your name."

"I didn't throw it." The young man sassed.

"Wow." SaeKu nodded, noting that he'd stolen one of her lines. "Classic."

"I've waited a long time to say that shit. Y'all females do it all the time."

"We do!" SaeKu couldn't help but be truthful.

"Let me get this bag, and I'll follow you."

"Okay." SaeKu allowed him to grab her suitcase, and then took off.

"Jax."

"Huh?" SaeKu questioned, looking back.

"My name is Jax. Yours?"

"I'm SaeKu."

"SaeKu?"

"Yeah. Like, Say – Ku."

"That shit mad sexy, yo. No disrespect."

"None taken." SaeKu smiled. "Here we are, a corner and a hung right later."

The little corner end bar that SaeKu had accepted the invitation to was spilling with patrons. Her head began to spin at the thought of waiting to be served. Dido was heavy on her mind, and she guessed that Jax could read through the lines.

"I wasn't expecting this shit to be jamming like this." He pulled his slightly baggy jeans up over his ass, only for them to slide back down a bit.

"Me either."

"Hold up!" he held up one finger, leaving SaeKu's bag at her side, he walked into the small space. After a few seconds, he waved the bartender over to where he was standing. She ignored the costumers hooting for her attention to assist the handsome black man with the one dimple in his cheek. SaeKu watched as he called off an order to her. Just a second later, she returned with two drinks in hand. Jax went into his denims and pulled two hundred dollar bills from his knot, and handed them to her. Winking, he turned and headed back to SaeKu.

Dope boy, she thought as she smiled and accepted the drink that he'd given. *Not interested.*

"Better?"

"Much! What's this?"

"I have no idea. I told the bartender to give me the girly drink. I'm sipping Crown."

"You just assumed that I wanted the girly drink?" SaeKu frowned.

"Being that you had to take a breather after the first sip, I think that my assumptions were right. You're not a drinker. Don't hate. Give me my props. I called it."

"Alright. You did." SaeKu admitted. "I don't really…"

"Hold up." Jax held his hand up and listened to the speaker over the intercom. "Damn."

"What?"

"That was the last call for my plane." He hissed. "Let me see your phone." he demanded. Before SaeKu could decline, he was snatching it from her hand. He quickly punched his digits in, and turned his cup bottom side up. Finishing off his drink, he dumped it in the trash next to SaeKu. His cell rung and then, he handed her back her phone.

"I'll see you around, SaeKu. I'd say our first date at the corner bar was pretty cool. Brief, but we can worry about the specifics another time. I have to be out." Jax lifted his hand to salute SaeKu.

She was left with her drink in hand, not bothering to take off as soon as he did. She hadn't known how much she could use the beverage until it was sliding down her throat. Immediately, thoughts of Jax's existence ceased, and SaeKu sent Dade a text to let him know that she wanted Dido ready when she made it. Before finishing off her drink, she felt a vibration, signaling that he'd texted back, but she didn't bother to check.

**

As planned, Sage and SaeKu took the girls to Philly a bit before they'd initially planned. It was refreshing to see their people, again. The children were all squared away with Mason and Raven before they bid the crew farewell. A day of hardcore pampering pursued, leaving the women to nap before rejoining for the party later that night.

"SaeKu!" KinZu screamed from the doorway. "Why aren't you up and getting ready?"

"What time is it?" SaeKu sluggishly raised from the spare bedroom that she claimed each time she was in town. Without waiting for a response, she grabbed her cell to check the time.

She'd surprisingly received a call and text from an unknown number. Glancing at her clock, she realized it was a little pass nine. The girls had plans of meeting up before the extravaganza, but SaeKu wasn't certain that she'd make the prior turn up. She'd overslept, needing the rest more than anyone knew.

"Aw shit." She cursed, stretching her arms and yawning. "I'm getting up. I may not make the little thing or whatever. I was dead ass tired."

"I see. Maybe you should lay back down. The party doesn't end until the wee hours. We're just meeting up to have a little private affair before the big affair."

"No, I'm fine. I need to get up. I'm glad you were here to wake me, or I would've missed the entire show."

KinZu stared at her younger sister from the hallway. She buckled her earrings into her ears as she admired her. Time was on her side, and she was aging beautifully. Dido's entrance into the world had helped SaeKu discover herself, and KinZu couldn't have been prouder.

"Yeah, you were pretty much out of here." KinZu chuckled. "Well, I'll be leaving soon enough. If you're ready, then you can tag along. If not, then I will see you soon."

"Okay. I'm telling you now, I'll be a minute. I'm sure Sage is just as behind as I am, so I'll grab a ride with her."

"Okay."

SaeKu stood from the bed, and skipped to the bathroom. She relieved her bladder, and returned in minutes. Her cell chimed, alerting her of a message. She was quickly reminded of the one that she'd already had. Of course, Sage was letting her know that she was running behind schedule. SaeKu let her know that she had the same case, and was sure to tell Sage that she'd need a ride from KinZu's house.

"Okay SaeKu. It's show time." she gave herself a prep talk.

Back in her message app, she tapped the message from the unknown number. As she'd thought, it was the guy Jax that she'd met two days prior. He'd sent a simple, *What's good?* With his name tagged at the end of the message. SaeKu didn't bother responding. She just wasn't interested. Instead, she connected her Bluetooth to KinZu's speakers, and opened Pandora.

Beyoncè's "Sorry," blasted through the speakers as she sung along, bouncing up and down as she made her way to the closet. She pulled out her desired attire, and went to work. By the time an hour had rolled around, she resembled something from the front page of a magazine.

Chapter Three

Meek had brought the city out for his New Years celebration. Everyone was primped and primed, looking like they belonged on the cover of magazines. The crew was thick and moved heavily in the building. Their section was stocked, entirely, with the best bubbly, brown, and any liquor that the club owner even though they would consume.

"SAGE!" SaeKu yelled over the blaring sounds of Jeezy's Trap Anthem.

"Huh?" Sage finally paid enough attention to answer to SaeKu.

"I've been calling your name for some time. Where the hell is your head?"

"Girl, on my chucks that I left in the car. I swear. Lorde hasn't shown yet, but I have a feeling I'll be needing them by the time the last record spins." Sage rolled her eyes into the ceiling.

"Why would you say that?" Wise leaned over and asked.

"Because, this nigga gets foolish. His eyes love to roam, and I am not for the disrespect tonight." Lorde was turning Sage into someone that she could barely identify with.

As of lately, she'd been having a sinking feeling that his extra curriculum activities were unpleasing to their relationship. He'd been moving funny, and she'd taken notice. Her intuition was never far fetched, but she prayed that she was highly mistaken this one time.

"Their eyes are going to roam. If not, then I would think that my nigga was fruity. Now, if that dick roams, then we can all go to the trunk. You aren't the only one with a pair of spares in the whip." Bella sipped her drink, bouncing to the beat as she scanned the crowd for Kelly. She would be arriving at any minute.

"Right. Now, that's when we have a problem. Enjoy yourself. Don't let the night pass you by worried about a man that isn't going anywhere." Reed shrugged, and sipped on her sprite.

Keem had her on a no liquor diet. Their son, RaKeem Jr, was still feeding from her breast, so she had to tread lightly.

Nodding her head, Sage agreed with everything that the girls were saying. Turning back towards the crowd, she peeped over the balcony that they were seated on, and allowed the atmosphere to consume her.

"I need to go to the restroom." SaeKu admitted, drawing Sage's attention once more.

It was forbidden to stray away from the crowd alone, so Sage gathered her bearings to move in sync with her bestie. SaeKu stood from the velvet sofa, stretching her long legs in the process. The skin tight one-piece bodysuit that she wore showed her assets –ones that she'd acquired through pregnancy. Her thighs had thickened, and her butt hung over the back of her legs. She'd stressed in the gym about losing the baby weight, but the strenuous exercising did nothing to held rid the of the hips, breasts, and ass that she'd gained.

The champagne colored ensemble was covered with sequin at the top, and cuffed her ankles before leading to the matching Gucci pumps that she'd purchased the day before. As of lately, she'd been rocking a sleek bob that was cut right under her chin. The young and gullible SaeKu had grown into a fierce MILF with a serious sex appeal to match. Sage trailed behind her as she started for the stairs.

With a nude Dior dress that tugged at her curves, Sage looked flawless. Bella had touched everyone's face, enhancing their beauty. Her hair was in big loose spirals that often fell into her face, causing her to push them backwards. The shimmery highlight that Bella had patted onto her checks had Sage glowing, shining every time she smiled.

"You good?" SaeKu asked once they'd dispensed from the crew.

"You ever just had this feeling?" Sage questioned.

"What feeling?"

"Like something just wasn't right." Sage saddened.

"I have. Is that why you're no fun, tonight."

"I think Lorde is cheating on me." She blurted, causing SaeKu to buck her eyes as they continued through the crowd.

"Why would you say that?"

"He's been a little distant lately. Plus, I just feel it. Something is off."

"Maybe you're over thinking it. Has he given you any reason to question his loyalty?"

"No. Not lately."

"Okay, then. There you have it. Until he gives you a reason, then don't worry your pretty little head."

"Maybe you're right." Sage shrugged as they reached the ladies room.

"Don't make something be wrong when it's not. Lorde tends to the streets. There's no telling what is going on out there that has him acting a way."

"You're right." Sage agreed, again.

"Let's just enjoy the night, and continue this conversation when we get back home –or not at all." SaeKu smiled, and kissed her friend on the cheek. Before walking away, she patted her on the ass, making it jiggle.

"So gay." Sage chuckled.

"Only for you my love." SaeKu blew Sage a kiss, and then disappeared into the first empty stall.

**

Dade squinted his eyes to adjust to the dark setting of the club. Before stepping into the crowd, he surveyed his surrounding. Lorde was at his left using the same tactic before they moved in unison. It was a habit, survival on the street had taught them well.

Dressed in all black, Dade wore a tailored suit that hugged his biceps and abdomen area. Much like SaeKu, the gym had become his closest friend. The stresses of his everyday life had driven him to release. He was, now, rock solid and full of muscle.

"AYO." Dade heard and turned to the sound of familiarity.

None other than RahMeek Jones was beckoning for his attention as he stood near the front of the club, speaking with a staff member. Two hops and a skip away, Dade and Lorde was upon him within second.

"Y'all niggas sliding through this bitch looking like new money." Meek whistled, patting Roc in the chest. "Check out these clowns."

"What's up, nigga?" Roc embraced Dade.

"This my brother Lorde. Lorde, this is Meek and Roc. You niggas done met, just not face to face."

"Yeah, big homie already family." Meek shook up with Lorde, and then Dade.

"Y'all nigga must thought we were going to church?" Lorde questioned, realizing everyone was suited except for him. "Cause, last time I check a motherfucker said we were heading to a party. Y'all in this bitch with wedding suits and shit on."

"Nigga, don't knock us because you missed the memo. I told you black tie attire. That ain't mean black jeans and a fucking tee."

"Nigga this a dress shirt." Lorde wanted credit for his Armani Exchange top. He had decided to go all out for the party, and Dade was trying to handle him like he wore that shit on the daily.

"You know damn well that ain't no dress shirt. That's a V-Neck." Roc called Lorde out on his shit.

"V-Neck. Crewneck. Whatever neck nigga." Lorde hollered back.

"You could've at least wore a button down." Dade laughed.

"Na. I can't move in that shit. I feel too restricted. You never know when shit may get sour and you need some elbow room." Lorde started flexing in his shirt. "Bet you niggas can't even reach for your waistline without busting one of them buttons."

"If I can't reach for it, my bitch can. She ready at all times." Meek boasted, pulling the toothpick from his mouth.

"Damn, what kind of bitch you got?" Lorde question, thrown back by Meek's response.

"Chill on the disrespect."

"Well… shit… I thought because you… Then I…" Lorde tossed his hand in the air. "Fuck it." He felt where Meek was coming from, because it would be hell to pay if a nigga ever disrespected Sage like that.

"The kind every man needs at his side." Meek answered his question. "You gentleman ready to skate out?"

"Born ready." Roc straightened his suit jacket, and the four men started through the club, stopping when noticing Keem coming their way.

"Big money Keem." Roc joked.

"Whatever nigga. I'm going to loan you my tailor's number because yours fucked that fitting up." Keem checked Roc really quickly. "That color doesn't even fit your skin type."

"Ole gay ass nigga. I'm going to have to tell little sis to watch out for your ass."

"Oh trust me…" Keem boasted. "Little sis knows this dick is only for her."

Keem stepped out of Roc's reach, immediately. He was no fool, and knew that his words had struck a nerve. Even up in age, Roc still considered Reed his baby girl. They were two children in, and he had yet to acknowledge the fact that they were married and sexing on the regular.

"Y'all nigga need to chill." Meek chuckled, knowing the two would be at it all night.

The club-goers became motionless as they gawked over the men of the hour. Fellas pulled their women closer, and women that had come out with intentions on snagging a big spender mouths watered with lust and desire dripping from their lips.

Strolling, the crew all had their sights set on the area reserved for their celebration. The feeble minded females that attempted to entice them, and the crusty ass niggas that were desperate for a hand shake were overlooked and unheeded. When they reached their designated area, Dade's eyes darted through the darkness in search of his once passionate lover. Her absence startled him, stirring questions within his mental. As the rest of the men crowded their women's space, Dade was left to wonder where his baby mother was.

"Where the fuck Sage ass at? She done got one of them new wigs, and I guess the beautician glued that shit to the part of her head that helps her to think. She knew damn well to be here when I got here." He barked.

At the realization that Sage was missing as well, Dade's anxiety calmed. No, he wasn't truly apart of SaeKu's life, except for them sharing a daughter together, but he felt as if she was indebted to him −mentally, physically, and emotionally. Although he'd come from off of his SaeKu high after learning of the attempted abortion, that hadn't changed the sense of pride and ownership he deemed over her life. For this, she'd labeled him as the baby father from hell, but he didn't give two shits.

"Sage is going to get fed up, and beat you across that bald ass top of yours." Dade chuckled.

The vibration of his cell in his pocket removed his thoughts from the spiraling conversation, causing him to dig in. He checked the caller's identification before deciding to answer. Plugging one finger in his ear, he placed his cell at the other.

"Yo."

"Hey. I'm out front." Claudia's smile could be heard over the loud music thumping through the speakers of the club.

"Aight. Give me 30 seconds, and I'll be out to get you."

Dade ended the call, giving one more quick sweep of the VIP section before taking the steps two at a time. He'd invited one of his bed's latest frequenters to the showdown to have a good time. Claudia had just finished medical school, and was in her last year as a Resident. She was the poster girl for the suburbs, and carried herself like a queen.

However, she got down with the roughest men of the city. She'd once admitted that dating men of her caliber was boring, and she'd tried it before knocking it. Although she refused to immense herself in the life of the men she dealt with, the daily risks they took were thrilling to her.

Dade stepped into the cold as fog formed clouds of smoke each time he exhaled. Claudia was nearing the black velvet rope wearing a smile that could light up the night. She was dressed to kill in a black mink mini coat that stopped above her waist. She sported a miniskirt that was covered with sparkles, and sheer top that left little to the imagination.

Dade's dick stretched against his slacks at the sight of the elongated human Barbie. Claudia's orange undertone turned beat red as she opened her arms and wrapped them around his neck. Dade inhaled the Chanel perfume that lingered on his pillow often.

"I missed you." Claudia sang in his ear. Covering her unpleasant touches, she rubbed Dade's manhood through his pants, and whispered. "You too."

Pulling back, Dade composed himself, and smiled. "Let me get you out of the cold." He replied, grabbing Claudia's arm, and leading her inside of the club. Bystanders that were waiting to gain access to the club hooted and whistled in silence as the couple made their entrance.

"If you even THINK I'm around, you need to be around, too." Lorde was spitting that dumb shit as Sage and SaeKu crowded back into their section. Sage couldn't help but to smile at the thought that her baby had been missing her, because she'd been missing him as well.

"Or what, nigga? If you miss me, then say it." Sage warned, leaning in to hug Lorde. "You can let your guard down, boo. It's me." Sage whispered into Lorde's personal space.

When she attempted to step back, Lorde pulled her back in. Grabbing her by the back of her neck, he covered her lips with his. The two tongue tangled, not bothering to take note of the others that were in the vicinity.

"I'm fucking you when we leave. Gone get you something to drink. That pussy be sloppy when you're full of it." Lorde slapped Sage on the ass.

"Good, because I've been fantasizing about sitting this drunk ass pussy on your face all day."

"Sage." Lorde looked her in the eyes. "I love you and all of that, but you're not just going to be testing my gansta with that sit on my face shit. You can't be just telling me shit like that."

"But it's the truth. You acting like I don't."

"Yeah, but don't ever mention that shit, aight?"

Sage cackled, causing Lorde to laugh to. He hated the fact that Sage brought every ounce of freak out of him. Whatever she wanted to do, he was down for it. The two had explored with one another since the day they'd become seriously involved, and he was loving every minute of that shit.

"You seen him?" SaeKu squatted on the cushioned booth next to Bella, who was perched on her husband's lap. She knew that she could get info from her sidekick.

"Ummm Hmmm." Bella nodded, accepting the drink that RahMeek was handing to her. It seemed as if it was the men goals to get their spouses drunk before having a fuck fest.

Rolling her eyes, SaeKu hated even the sound of that. "He was looking for you, too."

"Really?" SaeKu mumbled.

"Well. I think…" Bella's sentence was cut short as she watched Dade approach the section –once again. This time, he was accompanied by a wig wearing, artificial blonde. "Yeah. I was wrong." Bella realized who Dade was searching for through the dimness of the club.

"This nigga." SaeKu grabbed the spiked drink from Bella's hand, and threw it back.

She needed another one the minute it was gone. Bella was on it, tapping Meek's leg to make another one. He followed suit. Bella continued to watch Dade barge through their section with his bitch as she passed the cup to SaeKu.

"You might need something a little stronger than this." Bella urged as the blonde nearly undressed in front of everyone's eyes. She was wearing a bad ass two piece, summoning the attention of even the married men amongst her.

SaeKu's eyes met Dade's as he smiled and nodded. His nonchalant attitude shot daggers through her chest as she watched him maneuver through the VIP introducing his companion to the entire crew. His final stop was at the booth that she, Bella, and Meek occupied. After shaking up with Meek and Bella giving him the cold shoulder instead of a hug, Dade was amongst her.

"Claudia, SaeKu. SaeKu, Claudia." He stated, just like that.

There was no sign of significance as he introduced her as another part of his posse. Not once did he mention the fact that she'd mothered his child and swallowed a few –to say the least.

"Nice to meet you." Claudia reached out to SaeKu. Unlike Bella, she found her manners, and shook hands with the beautiful young woman who was clinging onto her baby's father for dear life.

"Likewise." SaeKu nodded, barely able to emit the words from her mouth.

There was no way in hell that she could front like she wasn't fucked up behind Dade's actions. It was as if he was on a quest to tear her from the bottom up. Everyday, he lived to make her life a living hell, while he lived carefree. Even though SaeKu loved Dido to death, she wondered where they would be had she never been born. If Dade didn't have direct access to her life, would he treat her like the scum of God's green earth. Would he had forgiven her just as God, and the two went their separate ways? Or would time had mended their broken hearts, and pulled them closer together?

Grabbing SaeKu by the hand, Bella began to rock her hips. "Come on, ladies." She removed SaeKu from the burning furnace that she'd been placed in. "Let's get on this dance floor."

"We need to make a detour first." Wise announced, lifting from her husband's lap. "Ladies' room."

Liam had been at the club since the ladies had arrived. He didn't give a damn about teaming up with the other guys. There wasn't a chance in hell he was leaving his wife to roam the Philly club without him at her side. Nigga's were crazy, and he wanted to be right there if they ever got out of line. Besides, anything could happen. He didn't want to get caught slipping, leaving his wife to fiend for herself in the event of an unpleasant situation.

"We're right behind you." Everyone grabbed hands as they made their way down the stairs. Dade watched as SaeKu carefully took each step, being sure that she didn't fall.

When the women all made it to the restroom, there was one stall that was occupied. Beating on the door, Wise directed the occupant to vacate, immediately. "There's been an emergency, and they're clearing out the whole joint."

Kelly pressed her arm over her mouth to keep from laughing. The young lady didn't bother to wipe her ass as she scrambled to get out of the stall. Her pants were falling from her ass when she emerged, running for the door. Reed followed behind her, locking the door the minute she was out.

Everyone broke out into laughter, not believing what Wise had just done.

"What am I supposed to do?" SaeKu became serious. She wasn't feeling the emotional rollercoaster that life had been taking her on.

"Fight BITCH!" Bella screamed, jerking her head back as if this was supposed to be understood. "Oh. Maybe that's just me." she toned it down, realizing she was bat shit crazy over her husband.

"Over a man that doesn't even want my ass?" SaeKu could never.

"Exactly." Reed chimed in, causing everyone to look her way. "My bad."

"Ewwwww. Chile. Have my drink." Kelly handed SaeKu her drink, and she threw it back, too.

"He wants you." Wise cleaned the lip gloss from her lips, only to reapply more. "He's just too busy convincing himself that he doesn't to see it. Maybe not today or even next year... But he will come to his senses. Look how long it took you."

"Exactly, but we're not talking about that right now." Bella was hype. "I'm saying... What you about to do about this bitch with your man?"

"That is not her man!" Everyone yelled in unison.

"Y'all know what the hell I mean." The banging on the door didn't phase either f them. They continued their conversation.

"Don't give her another drink. I swear." Kelly laughed. "Meek is going to have fun with you, tonight."

"Meek has fun with me every night." Bella did a lite swirl, boasting.

"I bet." Kelly turned her attention towards SaeKu. "I say you get the nigga back. Don't let him see you feeling no type of way about this shit. Keep it 100, and be a little easy on the next nigga that tries to snatch you up." She shrugged.

"Exactly." Sage high-fived Kelly.

"Boss up on his ass." Sage gave her two cents. "You see what he's on. I know how hard it is, but scratch the thought of you two being together. Life just doesn't see things y'all way. In the meantime, don't put your life on hold while this nigga lives as free as a bird."

"She has a point." Bella nodded. "But..."

"No but." Kelly grabbed Bella by the lips and almost started a fight.

"Look, I love you to death but don't ever put them dick beaters to my face, again!"

Bella gripped Kelly's hands with enough force to move a MACK truck. Although Kelly was in pain, she couldn't contain the laughter that spilled from her lips. As Bella aged, she was becoming more of a live wire. Their time spent together was of pure joy.

"Come on, because Lorde breaking through this door... Locked and all if he can't find me for too long." Sage rounded up the ladies to leave.

As everyone gathered on the dance floor, Rihanna's, "Sex With Me," began to spin. SaeKu was feeling overly good with the three drinks in her system. She'd grabbed another from the bar as they maneuvered their way to the floor.

Bending over, she was sure to hold her cup steady. Singing along to the lyrics, SaeKu lifted up and rocked her hips from one side to the other. Holding her drink in the air, she grinded her body to match the beat perfectly. Just like clockwork, a gentleman slid behind her, placing his hand around her hip.

Fortunately for him, tonight, SaeKu was feeling a little generous. Opening her eyes, she was given a thumbs up by Wise – letting her know that the man behind her was a winner. He would get the job done. Tuning everyone out, SaeKu became lost in the lyrics of Rihanna's song, remembering the last time that she'd experienced sex as amazing as the kind that Rihanna referenced in her song.

Sure enough, it was with her child's father. The one who was staring holes into her skin from their section. Dade was unaware that Claudia was attempting to get his attention. She needed to use the ladies room, and wanted to be sure that she let him know where she was running off to.

"DADE!" she yelled.

"Uh… What's good?" he asked, using all of his strength to tear his eyes away from SaeKu as she grinded on some nigga's dick as if they were long lost lovers.

"I need to go to the restroom. I'll be back." Claudia informed.

"I'll be right here." Dade assured her, and patted her on the ass before she walked off.

Just as soon as Claudia was out of sight, Dade was on his feet to get a better view of the madness that was being created before his eyes. His knuckles turned red as he gripped the railing with force. SaeKu was trying his patience, and he had little to feed from as of lately.

"See." Lorde stood beside Dade to dissect the situation at hand. It didn't take a rocket scientist to know that he was fuming over his baby mama. "Sage is damn near in the corner. She's warding off any nigga that even look like he wants his life, tonight. But SaeKu… She's a single lady, man. You did that." Lorde was being honest. "Whatever that is down there… You created that. A motherfucker once told me to put my pride aside and go for what I loved. That same motherfucker letting his ego push him out of his own damn head."

"Yo." Meek walked up before Dade could respond to his brother. Out of all the years he'd grown with Lorde, it was the first time he actually made sense. "This nigga ain't said shit but the truth." Meek had overheard their conversation. "You come prancing some bitch through here bad enough to make every nigga in her path's dick stand, and expect that shit to sit well with SaeKu. Bella her motherfucking friend. I'm surprised this shit ain't came to blows."

"That's ain't SaeKu's memo."

"You're lucky, then." Meek whistled. "But to keep shit one hundred with you. If SaeKu kicks back even one more drink, little homie fucking tonight." The sound of Meek's statement had Dade's ears hot like lava. "And that pussy pleasing would be on your hands. We all know that drunk pussy is the runner up to pregnant pussy." With that, Meek walked off.

Looking towards the steps that Claudia had just descended, and the dance floor where SaeKu was allowing a nigga to touch all over her goodies, Dade made a rapid decision. Shrugging, he patted Lorde on the back and told him to watch his back.

"Nigga. I've got your front, back, side, side, above, below. All that shit."

"Roc." Dade signaled for Roc to follow him.

Philly niggas grimy. They'd try to do you dirty when you weren't looking. Real niggas took it to the face. There wasn't no sneak shit. Dade could hold his ground, but there wasn't any telling how many niggas this clown had with him, and how silly SaeKu was going to jump. Dade figured if he had to snatch SaeKu's ass up, he'd need a second set of hands if a nigga tried to get slick. During emotional warfare, all hell could break loose. Dade would be sitting in a cell after deading a nigga in a club full of witnesses about his bitch.

Dade slid through the crowd with hatred in his heart. He hated that he was about to have to step out of character, showing SaeKu what he was truly battling on the daily. He hated the way that she had so much power over his mind, body, and heart. He hated how his every move was dictated by her perceived reaction. He hated that gravity had forced them apart when all he wanted was for them to grow old together. He hated that even after all they'd done to one another, he still couldn't get enough of her. He hated the smile on her face as she allowed some stranger to caress his favorite canvas. He hated that SaeKu was enjoying every moment of the shit. He hated that he wished it was him that she was skillfully rotating and gyrating on. Most of all, he hated how if it came to it, he was willing to pop a nigga and go sit down for a bid for her.

Dade could not find the words to say to SaeKu as he approached her. He was so slick with it that the girl's hadn't even had chance to warn her of his arrival. Before he could control himself, he had his hands around her neck.

"What the fuck you supposed to be doing?" his vocal cord began to work.

"Nig…" her dancing partner straightened up and attempted to make a move on Dade.

"Bitch if you knew better, you'd try that shit on someone else." Dade gave the guy a menacing look, then focused back on SaeKu. "So you just like being disrespectful and shit?"

"Dade." She swallowed, becoming angrier by the second.

"Let my neck go!"

"Or what?" he taunted.

"Or…" the guy started, again.

"EWWWW. WEEEEE. Nigga. I wish. Na. Nigga. I encourage." Roc rubbed his hands together, stepping closer to Dade.

"See that." Dade turned and pointed to the red beam that was posted on the nigga's chest. "Don't make the wrong move and have Lorde splatter your shit. That nigga trigger happy, and had a list of corpse in his pocket that he's dying to add to."

They guy's eyes bucked as he began to look around the club to see where the red beam was coming from. He had no such luck. His eyes fell back upon Dade, and then over to Roc.

"This me all day and night, Joe." Dade kept it Philly. "When you see this, turn your head the other way."

"Or that." Roc pointed at Kelly. "That for sho." He pointed to Bella. "Or that." Reed shook her head. "Especially that." He pointed to Sage. "Or that." His eyes bulged when speaking about Wise.

**

"Let me the fuck GO!" SaeKu yelled through the parking lot of the club. The girls were on her trail, but standing a safe distance. Her pumps were scrubbing the ground as she tried to keep up with Dade. He was much too fast for her.

"I'm jumping in if she asks us." Bella was removing her jewelry as they continued behind Dade and SaeKu. Sage followed suit.

"Shut the fuck up!" Dade jerked her backwards before throwing SaeKu on the car. He was so frustrated with her that it didn't make much sense. She had his head gone, and he couldn't give the slightest reason why. The fact ate at him everyday, which is why he made her suffer the way he did. They were torturing each other.

"DADE!" SaeKu yelled, having the girl take notice of her emotional state. "Let me go!"

"You gone learn how to show a nigga some fucking respect."

"Respect? Respect?" SaeKu reached back and smacked Dade across his handsome face.

WHAM

"Nigga." SaeKu took off, throwing jab after jab.

On reflex, Dade jacked her up, and attempted to slap some sense into her. Bella was quick with it, grabbing his hand before it could connect with her face. "I wish the fuck you would." She dared.

SaeKu took the opportunity to continue to rain blows over Dade's face. She was paying him back for old and new. The women all stood to the side as she handled her shit. Dade didn't grab ahold of her hand until after a few seconds. Her face was flushed with tears as she cried out for him to stop making her life a living hell.

"Just leave me alone, Dade!" she pleaded. "You don't fucking want me, so what you expect me to do? Huh? Crumble and die? Just stop it. I hate the day I met you!"

"Shut up!" he grabbed her face, squeezing her jaws together. Her last statement had burned his chest something awful.

He hated to hear her sound so defeated. He didn't want to acknowledge the guilt that he felt for making her feel like she didn't mean shit to him, when she was his entire world. At the sound of her voice, Dade knew that she had given up. He'd tried breaking her, and succeeded. However, that wasn't what he wanted, not anymore. Dade wanted her to fight, fight for their love like he once had.

"You can do whatever you want, just keep that shit away from me!" he yelled into her face furiously.

"Dade." He heard from behind.

"Aw bitch. Go back inside." Bella knew who had come out without even having to turn around.

"Let's roll, Claudia." Dade advised, opening the door to his car, attempting to shove SaeKu inside.

"Aw hell nawl." Sage was outdone. She started for the car, but was snatched backwards.

"That's them folk's business." Lorde pulled her in the opposite direction. Following suit, everyone snatched up their women, and tugged them towards their vehicles.

"Get in the car." Dade yelled at SaeKu.

"NO!" SaeKu became lightheaded as she wobbled back and forth. "Move."

"SaeKu. Get in the fucking car. Damn. All our people waiting on us to be out."

"I'm riding back with Sage."

"Lorde ain't letting you in. Get in!"

SaeKu felt the urge to vomit, all of a sudden. Leaning over, she allowed the contents of her stomach to fall onto the ground. Dade, quick on his feet, moved back just in time.

"Dade. If she's getting in the front, then where am I supposed to be fitting?"

"In the back." Dade clarified what Claudia seemed to not understand. "I have to get my baby mama to her room, first."

"Baby mama?" Claudia shrieked.

"Yeah. Get in Claudia."

"Bu…"

"GET IN!" Dade yelled, not up to dealing with two hard headed bitches at the same time.

"SaeKu, get in the car before I throw you in this motherfucker." Dade had never used so much profanity in all of his days.

"No!"

"Aight."

Dade loved SaeKu's dirty draws. There wasn't shit a little bleach couldn't cure, so he didn't care shit about her puking her guts out less than a minute prior. Swooping her up, bridal style, he shoved her in his front seat. Surprisingly, she was unable to put up a fight. Her energy had depleted, and she was near exhaustion.

Claudia remained quiet as they road to the Westin hotel. SaeKu had fallen asleep on the ride over –nearly the minute Dade had laid her on his front passenger seat. He was thankful that he didn't have to argue with her the entire way, but was worried about how she'd feel once she woke up the next morning.

Chapter Four

The trip to Philly left SaeKu exhausted, physically, emotionally, and mentally. Dade had some nerve pushing up on her when he was there with a bitch already. Rolling her eyes into the ceiling, SaeKu became mad at just the thought. Hadn't she been so full of liquor, she would've had it out with him. She thought back to that night, still not believing that she had consumed so much alcohol. Her cell chimed, alerting her of an incoming call.

"Yeah?" she answered without warning. "Dido. Please just close your eyes." Dido had been fighting her sleep for the past hour. SaeKu was ready for a nap herself, but couldn't get comfortable until Dido was finished nursing and she could rest on her stomach.

"You know, they say that if a man buys you a drink then you owe him a date."

SaeKu recognized the baritone immediately. It was the guy from the airport. While she didn't feel like being bothered, male attention was welcomed. She wasn't receiving it from Dade, so she guessed she'd better get over it and accept it where she could.

"Jax." She chuckled.

"Oh. She remembered my name. Aha." He joked.

"You're one of many jokes."

"When you lead a life as serious as mine, a laugh every now and again has proven to be beneficial. Ms. SaeKu." Jax sang, questionably.

"Yes."

"I was wondering if you mind me cutting the bullshit and getting straight to the point of this call."

"I would love that, Jax."

"Cool. I want you to join me on a date. Tonight. Seven. Wherever you'd like. Your choice, as long as it's within the limits of Philly."

"Hmmmmm." SaeKu pondered. Dido's care came to mind, immediately. Sage was off to work, and her only option was Dade.

"If I can make arrangements for my daughter, then I might consider."

"Might. Na. I don't need a might. That's too much like maybe. I need a definite."

SaeKu was struck by his charm. He was persistent, and she could appreciate that. After a long pause, she agreed. "Okay."

"Okay? That sounds a lot like yes!" Jax smiled on the other end, making SaeKu smile as well.

"Probably because it is."

"Well, alright. Seven it is. Send me details on where we're dining and I will see you later."

"Sure thing." SaeKu ended the call.

She'd surely need a nap, now. Especially if she had plans for later. Looking at the time, she realized she had six hours until her date. If she slept for two, she'd have more than enough time to get Dido squared away, and dressed.

At six-thirty, SaeKu was ringing Dade's doorbell. He opened, bare chested and footed. SaeKu swallowed the lump in her throat before speaking. Her eyes had a mind of their own, continuing to travel downward –yarning to take a peek at his dick through the gray sweats.

"Hey. I've got to get going. I brought extra milk, because she didn't eat before we left the house." SaeKu fired off, handing Dido to her father.

"I think someone had a poopy on the way over."

"She did." SaeKu chuckled. "I was saving that for daddy to clean."

"I see. Where you headed?" Dade questioned, admiring the fitted jeans and white shirt. The white shirt hugged her breast, while the jeans hugged the other more pleasurable areas.

SaeKu's throat tightened as she thought of a reason she'd be dressed to kill with her makeup slayed for the gawds other than to go on a date. Her thoughts failed her, but Dido's timely cry saved her.

"Dade, she's really hungry. Go ahead and get her settled in. I have to go." SaeKu turned and begin to walk off. "I'll call you two in a few hours. Should I come back to get her?"

"Hell yeah!" Dade shouted, petty as they came.

He had a feeling that SaeKu was being secretive, but let the thought roll off of his shoulder. Usually, he would've denied her the chance to come back for Dido, but he needed her to come through when she was finished doing whatever the fuck she was doing. This way, he knew when she had made it in, and hopefully from where. Call it cock blocking, but he was far from stupid. SaeKu was going to stir up some foul shit if she was on that foolishness.

"You with it." SaeKu yelled back, getting inside of her truck.

The minute SaeKu pulled off from Dade's place, she connected a call to Sage. She picked up on the second ring. "Hey."

"Sage!"

"Yeah, what's up, SaeKu?"

"If Dade happens to call you or go snooping, I am with you at a staff dinner or some shit. Aight?" SaeKu didn't need Dade snooping.

"Alright, but why? What's going on?"

"I have a date." SaeKu smiled. She was actually quite fond of the guy, Jax.

"Wait. I must be hearing shit. You have what?"

"You remember the guy that I told you I met leaving work?" SaeKu questioned.

"Yeah. The one at the bar?"

"No." SaeKu chuckled. "The one that took me to the bar!"

"Oh yeah. Same difference. I thought you weren't interested."

"I honestly don't think that was the case. I just instantly compare guys to Dade or either just have him in the back of my mind when they attempt at talking to me."

"Right, because I've seen some real saucy ass niggas that you've turned down. If I wasn't tied down I would've jumped their bones." Sage sucked her teeth. "Glad you're getting over that shit quick. Dade foul ass." Sage rolled her eyes, thinking about the turn of events in Philly.

"Exactly. Fuck Dade. I just don't need him in my business. I swear he will give me grief over this shit."

"You ain't never lied, but I've got you covered. Call me when you get home and tell me how the date went."

"I will."

"Have fun, SaeKu. Let your hair down, bitch!" Sage laughed, hysterically before hanging up the phone.

**

"Yo, I can't believe you chose this shit." Jax screamed to a dancing SaeKu.

As much as he would've loved to get a goof glimpse of her shaking it in the fitted denim that she rocked, he could barely move. The guard railing had been his best friend throughout the entire night. SaeKu couldn't just chose a fine diner or the latest movie to catch.

Out of all places, SaeKu had decided on the skating rink. Jax wanted to decline, but he hadn't realized where he was headed until he was pulling into the parking lot. He spotted SaeKu, instantly, looking scrumptious in the white and blue jean ensemble.

"You said wherever I wanted to go. Next time, be more specific!" she yelled as she flew by him for the hundredth time.

"This shit is for the birds." Jax sucked his teeth, figuring staying still was probably his best bet. He'd fallen three times, yet SaeKu controlled the floor with grace. She was so fucking beautiful that Jax wouldn't have mind chilling and watching her do her thing. In fact, that's exactly what he planned to do. As she neared him, again, she lifted her right leg and leaned it backwards –slowing down. Slamming into the guard rail, she smiled –showing off those perfect teeth.

"What happened? You were doing great out there! Did you never go skating as a kid?"

"Yeah, to get up on some little young hoes. Wasn't no nigga out here rolling around."

"My bad." SaeKu was in tears, laughing. "I thought everyone knew how to skate."

"Man, I ain't skated a day in my life. Niggas from the hood came to the rink for two things, to stunt and to rack up on some hoes. That's it."

"Oh my God. That's awful. I actually loved skating as a kid."

"Maybe it's a girl thing, because my little sister knows how to skate too. She loved that shit. She was my excuse to go on some weekends."

"Oh my God, you have a younger sister?"

"Yeah. I had a younger brother, too, but he got smoked out here bullshitting in these streets." Jax gritted his teeth, still heated from the death of his brother. Although his death was justified by the street code, he still hadn't come to grips with it. His murderer never boasted or bragged about the body he'd added to his list, but he was certain as to who the nigga was. He couldn't wait to catch him slipping either.

"I'm sorry to hear that." SaeKu held her hand to her chest.

"It's all good, me and Kass are all moms got, so I try to keep her on the straight and narrow. She's a good girl, though."

"That's good. I have an older sister. It's just us two. Do you have any children?"

"Na. Never really wanted any. I mean, it may happen one day, but children aren't something I'm in a rush for."

"I feel you on that one. I have a daughter, and I'm definitely in no rush for another one." SaeKu laughed. "But I love my baby girl to death."

"Word?" Jax witnessed the love within SaeKu's eyes.

"Yeah."

Jax's cell chimed, disturbing their intimate encounter. He stepped off of the floor and grabbed the nearest seat. SaeKu trailed behind him, resting her bones before going back out onto the floor. As Jax fired off at whoever was on the phone, SaeKu checked her own. She'd turned it on silent just in case Dade decided to make a mess of her night. As expected, she had a missed call and a text from him. As usual, he didn't want shit. Breathing deeply, she shoved her cell back into her pocket, and met eyes with Jax.

He was a very handsome young man. His hair was thick and wavy at the top with faded sides, and a smooth goatee. Unlike Dade, his was trimmed low –much like his hair. He had a grown man sex appeal to him, capturing SaeKu with his big button eyes. She could almost bet that he had to grow into them. Surely, those beautiful round browns didn't fit his face as a kid.

"Yo, I'm starting to think you have some man back home that has some type of spell over you. Every time I'm trying to get at you, somebody pulls me away." Jax smiled, showing that one dimple. SaeKu melted in her seat at the deadly combination –smooth skin, big eyes, goatee, fade, pearly whites, and a deep dimple.

"Maybe." SaeKu shrugged. "Or maybe you're just a busy man, and everyone demands a bit of your time."

"Maybe so." Jax shrugged. "I hate I'm dipping for the second time." he bugged.

"It's fine. It's not like we just got here."

"You're right, but I wanted to spend more time with you. I tell you what… This weekend, my sister is having a little get together at her crib. Well, not really. We eat together once a month just to check in with each other and touch basis. Since my brother left so suddenly, we try to keep ourselves as close as we can. I never even bring my phones inside. It's against the rules. I'd like it if yo joined me. That's cool?"

"I wouldn't want to intrude, Jax. It seems pretty personal to me."

"Na. You good."

"If you say so."

"I'll text you with the details. Let's get out of these skates, though. I'm going to walk you out to your ride."

"Okay."

**

Throughout the entire week, Jax had SaeKu floating on cloud nine. Twice, he had met her at the airport before work to have breakfast. Other than those brief moments together, the two caked on the phone like young teenage lovers. Her text thread was full of emojis and deep conversation. Slowly, he was waking something up inside of her that she had buried.

As time progressed and the two became more acquainted, SaeKu realized she had been fucking up by running potential boos off. Jax was the first that she'd even given a second thought, but she was glad that she had. Luckily, the situation with Dade was at the back of her mental –barely ever appearing unless in his face. Even then, sometimes, she was too busy with her phone to pay him much mind.

She'd questioned Sage about the rapid connection that she felt with Jax, but Sage assured her that it was just something new. She was feeling the jitters after being out of commission for so damn long. Hearing those words encouraged her to continue with the little fling just to see where it would lead. It was simple fun.

"You all dolled up and shit." Jax rubbed his hands like the rapper Baby, cheesing as SaeKu slammed her truck door. She'd just pulled up at his place. As promised, she was accompanying him to his sister's place for dinner.

"I put on my good clothes, today." SaeKu joked, stretching her arms wide to hug Jax.

When their bodies connected, she closed her eyes to savor the smell that emitted from his body. He pulled away so soon, leaving her desperate for a few more seconds. Jax chuckled as he moved out of SaeKu's grasp.

"I missed ya little feisty ass." He admitted.

"Ummmm. Hmmmm."

"Dead ass, son. You ain't hit a nigga up all day long. I was starting to worry that you wouldn't come."

"If I said that I was coming, then I meant it. Word is bond."

"You right about that shit. You ready to roll?"

"Yeah. Let me grab my purse."

Surprisingly, Jax's sister lived just three minutes from SaeKu's place. She kept quiet, not ready to out her living quarters to Jax as of yet, but she took note of the elegant taste that his sister must have had. Jax refused to allow SaeKu out of and into his black Beamer without his assistance, so she waited for him to open her door before stepping out onto the pavement. The two were inside of the garage, hand in hand they stepped onto the elevator.

"I've always loved these. Your sister has good taste."

"And I'm the one that has to foot the bill. These shits cost more than they're worth. I can't wait until this girl marries and get out of my pockets. She call herself getting a boyfriend. He sounds pretty decent. I'll see today, though."

"She's bringing him?"

"He's already here." Jax shrugged.

"Oh so, you were using me." SaeKu laughed. "So you wouldn't be the only one without a date or feeling like the third when, huh?"

"Something like that."

"How dare you!" SaeKu slapped Jax's arm as the elevator doors swung open.

"I'm just fucking with you. I invited you before she said she was having the nigga over. It's because of you that she even told him to be here."

"Oh." SaeKu nodded.

"See, you owe me an apology." Jax lead the way down the narrow hallway.

"My bad." SaeKu followed.

Her heels connected with the tile on the floor until they came upon the last door on the stretch. Without knocking, Jax jammed his key into the lock and twisted it. He opened the door, and waved SaeKu inside. Her eyes scanned the living area, immediately. Laughter could be heard from the patio, being that the door was open.

"Kassie!" Jax called out, beckoning for his sister's attention.

SaeKu remained in the same spot by the door, trying to pinpoint the familiarity of the voice that was heard howling in laughter. Her nerves rattled at the thought of it being Dade. He was the only one who's laugh stuck with her. It was so contagious, and always caused her to laugh shortly after.

Suddenly, the laughter ceased, and footsteps could be heard from a far. SaeKu was almost afraid to see who was coming. It wasn't long before she felt Jax arm tightened around her shoulder and neck area. Tension rolled off of his tongue as he acknowledged his sister's guest.

"Kassie, this what you on?" He gritted.

SaeKu couldn't help but to steal a peek at the scene before her. Her heart fell from her chest at the sight of Lorde. The smirk that he wore on his face quickly retracted once they made eye contact. Sage was the first person that came to mind. Her girl wasn't just overthinking this shit. Lorde was truly fucking off. SaeKu was ready to break bad, immediately, and do the bitch in that he was fucking on. However, it wasn't her that was in a committed relationship, it was Lorde.

"Yeah nigga, this what she on." Lorde boasted. "SaeKu, remove that nigga's arm from around your neck –right now. Pronto." Lorde demanded. "We don't associate with pussy, period. You foul for fucking with a fuck nigga."

Jax looked down to SaeKu, confused at the connection. "Na, that ain't my bitch. But because that's my kinfolks bitch, I'm bout to beat the shit out of your hoe ass just on the strength. I mean, if that was my girl, he'd do the shit, too." Lorde shrugged. "Square up, nigga." He was serious as a heart attack, removing his jewelry, and handing it to SaeKu, that's how close he'd gotten to the two.

"Aight. You still standing there like I ain't about to take this shit there. Kassie, stay put baby girl. If you move, I swear SaeKu gone light that ass up."

"What?" Kassie was confused. "What's going on?"

"Ya big lil brother had sticky fingers and I put them bitches to rest. Your other big lil brother can't seem to let the shit go. He's been feeling some type of way ever since."

"Lorde." Kassie begin to cry. "You… You…"

"Yeah. Yeah. Yeah. I've been letting this nigga slip through the cracks. I started busting you down hoping to catch this nigga slipping. Today is my lucky day. Ain't shit personal. It was all apart of the plan, my G."

"Nigga, I let them guns talk. Ain't no hoe in my blood. We can handle this shit in the streets. This my little sister crib."

"Na. Don't try to back out of this ass whooping youngin. You been flexing and shit, wanting my attention. I'm here nigga. You summoned the king, bitch. Let's go." Lorde threw the first blow, catching Jax in the jaw. He had no time to react before Lorde was connecting his fist to the other side of his face. Blood shot from his nostrils as his body collapsed to the floor.

"Fuck I ain't mean to knock you down. Get up. We gone make this shit fair." Lorde moved back, giving Jax space and time to get his shit together.

He turned towards Kassie who was running towards the back room. He was certain that she was going to call twelve. "SaeKu, please get that dumb bitch. She bout to have a nigga sitting in a cell." SaeKu wanted to disobey Lorde and his antics, but didn't want to see him behind bars. She put a move on it, catching Kassie by the hair just before she made it to her bedroom.

"Uh. Uh." She shook her head, wanting so badly to get a punch or two in, but refrained.

"Lorde. What is happening? Why would you hit him like that? He did nothing to you!"

"Kassie, please shut the fuck up!" Lorde howled. "I'm trying to fight him like a man. See. I'm even giving this nigga room to get up and he still taking forever."

Kassie was astonished. She'd never saw Lorde act so irrational. His behavior was borderline crazy. She knew that her best bet was to keep quiet and try her best to block out the sight of her brother, who was back on his feet.

"Come on!" Lorde lifted his fist to his face. Jax swung, lazily. Lorde dodged his swing, retracted his right hand, and socked soul to Jax's left jaw. The powerful blow caused a crackling noise to echo throughout the loft. SaeKu squeezed her eyes together, and ran to his rescue. As he fell to the ground, she was right there beneath him.

"Lorde. You should be ashamed."

"SaeKu, if you don't get the fuck up. You trying to comfort a nigga that won't even swing back. Let that nigga back up so that I can knock his hoe ass out again. I've been waiting on this, boy, and you won't even put up a damn fight. Disappointment." Lorde shook his head. "But I'm waiting. Get up!"

"You know what…" SaeKu raised up from the floor, and fixed her clothing. "I'm not about to stand around and watch this shit. You're foul Lorde."

"Na, you foul. The fuck you doing cheating on my brother?"

"Cheating? Motherfucker I am single. News flash."

"Girl, you better check yourself. Don't get beside yourself. If I didn't want to take the pleasure from Dade, I'd beat your ass myself. You should be ashamed. Out here whoring and that man at home with y'all child. I swear. Bitches will make you catch a case!" Lorde yelled.

"Really? Are you fucking serious?" SaeKu was back on her feet. "You the one that's cheating. YOU! Nobody else in here is in a relationship. You're cheating, and I can't wait to tell Sage!"

"SaeKu, you foul as fuck if you do!"

"Well, I guess I'm foul as fuck then, nigga!" SaeKu threw Lorde his chain, and pulled open the front door. She didn't give a fuck what went on after she left. She was headed home, and would uber to get her truck.

"Good nigga. That a boy. Get that ass back up!" she heard Lorde speaking to Jax. She rolled her eyes and stomped down the hallway. She wanted to scream, yell, and even cry. It wasn't her heartbreak that she was feeling, but the heartbreak of her best friend.

SaeKu wasted no time getting on her cell. She had to tell Sage, because this shit was just too fucking unbelievable.

"Sage, are you sitting down?" she asked when Sage picked up.

Chapter  Five

Lorde reclined the leather seats in his ride, placing both palms on his forehead. He was contemplating his next move, knowing that it would need to be his best. There was no doubt in his mind that SaeKu would run her mouth. His question was when. If he could just get a time frame, then he could plan accordingly. However, he had nothing to go on.

"She was handling business with a nigga." Lorde recited the words, trying to see how they sounded coming from his mouth. "Na." he shook his head.

"That bitch run one of my spots. Ain't shit going on like that. You need to stop believing everything these hoes tell you." He said next, waving his hands in the air for emphasis. "Na." he thought to himself. "SaeKu ain't just any hoe."

"FUCK!" he lunged forward. "What the fuck am I going to say?" he questioned.

With his fist planted under his chin, Lorde thought long and hard. He had an insanely distinct feeling about this situation, and knew that Sage would accept no bullshit from his lips. She'd given into him with the hopes of being handle properly, but h was handling her like a basic bitch. Fucking off was unacceptable, and Lorde knew the shit. But like any other man, he let his dick lead and he followed.

"I just got to keep the shit G with her." he shrugged. "I can't make the shit no worse trying to lie. I have to give it to her straight. I fucked the bitch on some get back shit."

Hissing, Lorde nodded, "That's all I can do. Keep that shit trill with her. Damn."

Locating his keys, Lorde shut down the car and headed for the house. His breathing was labored and deeply influenced by his frightened nature. If there wasn't anything else that he feared in the world, Sage leaving him was the deal breaker. He loved that girl more than the early morning sun, assuring him that he'd lived to see another day.

The night had blanketed the sky many hours prior. Lorde entered his kingdom, and searched for traces up an upset and confused Sage. He was at least expecting her to be posted in the kitchen, or even by the window. Nothing. Oddly enough, Sage was sound asleep in their bedroom with Pryce tucked into her chest.

Lorde, never been one to rationalize, was struck with a dose of reality at the notion that this could all be snatched from his reality if he continued on the bullshit ass path that he was headed down. He wanted to beat his own ass for getting caught up, and by SaeKu of all people. She wasn't some random that he could go against. Her word was bond, and Sage knew that she wouldn't bring her back shit but the truth.

Sneaking inside of the bedroom, Lorde bent over Sage's frame and pulled Pryce into his chest. She stirred in her sleep, but didn't wake. Sage rolled over onto her back, realizing Lorde was home. Wiping her eyes, diligently, she acknowledged his presence.

"Hey." She spoke in a sleepy tone, rolling back over.

"Hey. I'm going to lay her in the bed."

"Okay." Sage nodded, waiting for sleep to find her, again.

When Lorde made the other side of their doorframe, he blew out a sigh of relief. He'd survived the first few minutes within him home. He didn't pull in to his shit in flames, or walk in to a woman gone mad. Shit like that was better than surviving a day in the hood. Every man knew that a woman scorn could be the death of him.

Lorde got Pryce settled before preparing to shower. In the comfort of his privacy, he cleaned his wounds, nursing the cuts and scraps to his knuckles. It was a damned shamed. Jax was no match for a battle with him. If niggas in the streets knew how much of a hoe he was, then they wouldn't even respect him! He was a beefy ass nigga, known for starting shit. Lorde had been waiting for the day to knock his ass out, and he'd gotten his chance –and done so several times.

Lorde dried his limbs and replaced his street clothes with night clothes. When the light from the bathroom shined into the bedroom, he got a quick glimpse at Sage curled up in the fetal position, sleeping so peacefully. A smile stretched his lips wide as the Red sea, calming his body even more than the relaxing shower that he had just finished. Lorde shut the light off, and climbed in bed beside Sage. Pulling her deeper into his chest, he allowed sleep to invade his space. It was only minutes before he was down.

Clenching her teeth, silently, Sage fumed from below. Lorde had come into their home as if everything was kosher. Of course, SaeKu had dialed her digits the minute the fiasco had ceased. Lorde had acted a plum fool that night. What was even worse was that SaeKu had confirmed her suspicions with her own eyes. Lorde was indeed fucking off on her.

For the past three hours, Sage had tried to locate her thoughts, figure out her next move, or just gather herself for a second. Her insides were doing summersaults. Both upset and confused, she craved direction of some sort. Since a kid, she'd heard the stories of many women staying after their man knowingly cheats, but she had vowed to never be one.

As much as she loved Lorde, she would not be anyone's fool —especially after he'd fought so hard to get her. Sage figured he should've saved the energy to keep her. If there wasn't another thing she knew, she was certain that she would no longer be a resident of the home she was currently in by the following morning.

An hour would pass before she was removing Lorde's arm from her frame. Sage wanted to make sure that he was good and asleep so that she could put her plan in motion, one that she'd half-assed before he'd made it to their home. Once up, Sage slid into her slippers and turned for the door. Looking back at Lorde's frame, she shook her head with disgust.

Paddling down the hallway, she stopped at Pryce's bedroom. Once inside, she dipped below her bed, and flung the covers upward, kneeled down, and slid the large suitcase from under the bed. A woman of caution, Sage kept an emergency bag on hand at all times. There were enough clothes to last Lorde, Sage, and Pryce for an entire week within the bag –rolled military style with necessities in tow.

Standing back to her feet, she dusted herself off and sighed. Using her shoulder, she wiped a lone tear from her eyes. She refused to cry any longer. For the last three hours, she'd cried all that she would.

Instead of rolling the suitcase down the hall, pass the bedroom, Sage decided to carry it. If not, she'd run the risk of waking Lorde. It was the last thing that she wanted while trying to make her great escape. The overbearing suitcase caused a bit of a problem for Sage's small frame as she wobbled to the front door with it in her hand.

Pulling her cellphone from her pajama pocket, Sage silenced the alarm with her phone, careful not to make a ruckus. After being assured that all was cleared, Sage unlocked the front door and eased it open. She lifted the suitcase handle when she reached the concrete, and rolled it to her car. The doors had been unlocked all night, which was in an attempt to not wake Lorde as well. Sage stuffed their belongings in the backseat, and headed back into the house to get Pryce.

As she turned to shut the front door, a bright idea came to mind. She'd considered a million ways to hurt Lorde or return the heartbreak that he'd caused, but her only solution was leaving. Now, she had a more gratifying departure on her mental, and knew that she'd feel so much better leaving afterwards.

Tiptoeing into the kitchen, Sage grabbed two medium sized pots from the set that hung on their rack. She filled them both a quarter of the way before putting them on the stove. Hiking the temperature setting to high, she let the water heat up. Finding something to do with her time, Sage went under the cabinet and found the bleach. Luckily, she'd just gotten four fresh bottles for the remainder of the month.

Sage grabbed them one by one, and sat them on the counter. A scowl pursued her precious face as she unscrewed the top and poked a whole into the foil of the first bottle. The second bottle followed, and then so on. Sage's mind ran rapid as she prepared for her grand exit.

"Stupid ass niggas. I don't understand this shit. How could he…" Sage paused. "Don't even go there Sage." She found herself communicating with herself. It was weird, but niggas made you that way.

"He's going to learn, today, though. I bet you that." Sage nodded her head, agreeing to her own statement. "Stupid motherfucker!"

With two bottles of bleach in her hands, Sage left the kitchen. Through the carpeted hallways, she let the first bottle rip. Tilted to pour the perfect amount, Sage walked through the house bleaching the tan colored carpet with no regret. Living room, spare bedroom, game room, game station, pool table, bed sets, fabric headboards, and anything else that was bleachable, Sage attacked.

After a while, she pulled her shirt over her nose to block out the fumes. Bottle two ended back in the same hallway that she's started. Sage ran back into the kitchen to retrieve the second set. Instead of staying in the house, she slipped back out of the front door. Quiet as could be, she stationed the bleach bottles on the concrete within the garage. Going into Lorde's secret stash, she found his master key ring, and unlocked the doors to his Jeep, G-Wagon, and Ashton Martin.

"I won't need much." Sage noted.

First, she went for the Wagon. Inside, she chunked bleach on the driver side floor. The seats were leather, so there was no use. Leaning over, she tossed more onto the passenger floor mats, and the back mats were to follow. Each car received the same treatment, leaving Sage with a few splashed of bleach. The second bottle sat on the concrete, still. She grabbed it on the way back inside of the house. The next stop was the closet. Because they both had so many belongings, they'd turned a spare room into their walk-in closet.

Sage pushed the door open with a full bottle of bleach in one hand and a near empty one in the other.

She sat them both by the door before walking further into the closet. Sage was in turmoil as she yanked Lorde's clothing from the hangers. Her heart fell to the floor with each piece, tugging at her balance. It sickened her the way that his cologne invaded her nostrils against her will and brought tears to her eyes. Horror-struck, she allowed her cries to be heard while she continued in rage.

"Damn you, Lorde." She mumbled, tired out of her mind.

Looking around her, she had pulled the better half of his things to her feet. With the back of her hand, she wiped her face and stepped through the pile of expensive designer labels. Bending, Sage tilted the bottled over and soaked the high fashioned pieces, being sure to end with his shoes.

Sage chunked the empty bottles with the bleached clothing and stomped out with her fragmented heart still at her soles. By the time she made it back into the kitchen to survey the pots, the tad bit of water that she'd poured into them had evaporated.

"Perfect." She smiled. "Perfect."

Sage turned off the stovetop and grabbed the long handles of each pot. They were warm in nature, but her adrenaline didn't allow her to deter from the task. Sage rushed through the bleached hallway full force until she reached she and Lorde's resting place. Inside of their bedroom, she jumped onto the bed, clocking Lorde across his bald scalp with the pot in her right hand. The heated blow woke him from his sleep, immediately. Before he could react, she was hitting him again, the second pot landing on his shoulder.

"AH. Shit. What the fuck?" he questioned.

"You stupid BITCH!" Sage fumed, following behind Lorde as he jumped from the bed to put some distance between the two of them. His arms were in the air, blocking her from hitting him in the head or face –again. Sage didn't give a damn, she settled for the arms. She tore them up with the piping hot kitchenware.

"SAGE!" Lorde called, trying to get her attention. "What the fuck, yo? Is you crazy, girl?"

Over and over, she gave him body shots until her emotions and strength weakened, simultaneously. "What did I ever do to you?" she questioned Lorde couldn't bare the sight of her. Sage was broken, and he didn't need her teary eyes to confirm.

The last swing wasn't powerful enough to cause any damage. Exhausted, Sage dropped the pots, and turned on her heels. There was no use in putting up anymore fight. Her limbs were tired, and chest was burning. Shrugging her shoulders, she stumbled off like a drunk –for she was truly intoxicated and inebriated. Love had been the cause.

"Sage. Wait." Lorde yelled out to her, grabbing her by the right arm. Spinning her around to face him, his chest caved in and then propelled as he gazed into her eyes. She was so different, so inoperative.

"I'm leaving you."

"No. You can't. You can't leave me. Wh…"

"I'm leaving you, Lorde, and I'm taking my baby with me!" Sage yelled. "You sick son of a bitch. My heart… my soul… my time… my life… my love… my pussy wasn't enough for you! Huh? It just wasn't enough? You just had to go and do it, didn't you?"

"Sage!"

"I NEEDED you to prove me wrong!" She cried. "I needed you to exceed my expectations and make a full of my assumptions. Yet, you go and do exactly what I knew you would… Break my fucking heart, rip it from my chest, and stomp on the motherfucker."

"It wasn't even like that, Sage. Please, just listen."

"Listen? Listen? Why am I listening after the fact? Matter of fact… why are you just talking and trying to communicate after the fact? If there was something that I was lacking, then you should've been talking before now, asshole!" Sage pointed into Lorde's chest with her manicured nails.

"Sage, you got everything a nigga needs and more. It had nothing to do with you."

"Well what the fuck was your reasoning?"

"Just being stupid, ma."

"Look where stupid has gotten you!" Sage wanted so desperately to connect the palm of her hand with Lorde's face. "I fucking hate you!" she whimpered. "I did nothing to deserve this from you, Lorde. I…" she halted. "Nothing." She shook her head, wiping her tears.

"Sage! SAGE." Lorde called out to her. "SAGE. Don't just…

SHIT!" He fumbled with words.

Without warning, she took off into a sprint, going to get

Pryce. It was best that she left before she said things that she

regretted. The last thing she wanted to do was be pulled out of

character any more than she had already been. Lorde's footsteps

could be heard behind her.

"What the fuck?" he questioned, stepping into the wet

hallway with bare feet.

Sage felt a bit glorious, knowing that he was stuck. He

couldn't come behind her at least until he covered his feet. The smell

of bleach was potent, so she was certain that he had no questions

about the liquid. Besides, the carpet was no longer it's original color.

"Come on, baby." Sage patted Pryce on her back, upset that

she was even waking her up from her sleep.

"Sage. Put her down man. Let's talk about this." Lorde

pleaded from the opposite end of the hallway.

"Fuck you! We don't have shit to talk about!" Sage yelled back, tucking Pryce under the blanket that was sprawled across her crib.

"Look. I can clear this all up if you just..."

Sage walked towards Lorde full speed ahead. Her shoulder brushed his, pushing him backwards a bit. Before she was out of his reach, Lorde reached out and grabbed Sage by her long weave. Unfortunately for him, she was wearing a full wig, and still managed to slip from his tracks. While partially embarrassed, Sage continued in stride.

"What the shit is this..." Lorde shook his head, and took off after Sage. He wanted to laugh, but this was no laughing matter. He knew that by morning, she'd be pissed. Sage did not play when it came to her exclusive wig collection.

By this point, Lorde didn't give a damn about the bleach, burned skin, or the throbbing headache that was pending. All he wanted was to save face before Sage could completely leave his presence. Quick on his feet, he trailed behind Sage towards the door.

She was swift like the wind, catching him in the nose when she attempted to close the front door behind her.

"FUCK!" Blood rushed, causing Lorde to cry out. *This bitch is trying to kill a nigga, tonight.* He thought to himself, grabbing his nose –certain that it was broken.

The impact was so intense that it curated tears from his lids. His vision was blurred, but Lorde still managed to get out of the door, with his shirt pulled up to his face in order to soak up the blood flow.

"Sage." He hurried, barefooted. "Sage wait, DAMMIT!"

Like a thief in the night, Sage slid into her truck, dragging his entire life with her. Lorde made it to her door just before she was able to close it. With his arm stretched, he begged her to get out so they could talk.

"Please. Just come back inside. I can't even fight you right now cause you fucking me up. Don't leave like this!"

He tried staying firm, but in his heart he knew that it was a matter of time before he broke down like a bitch. At this point, his G status, street credit, and nothing else mattered. His bitch was pulling his card, one that was to forever remain in his hand.

"Lorde, I will run you the fuck down. Think I won't, nigga!"

I've created a demon. Lorde realized. In that moment, he knew that Sage had become the female version of himself. She loved so beautifully and so hard that she had every right to go ballistic when the regard wasn't held to the same extent.

"Come on baby, damn. I'm sorry, aight. But, don't just leave a nigga like that. We supposed to be in this shit together."

"You're absolutely right, Lorde, and I thought that we were. But, where were you tonight, huh? Where were you the night before that and two nights before that, huh?"

"Sage, let's not..."

"No! Let's do exactly that BITCH!" Sage was on fire sitting in her seat, tears running down her neck and chest area.

"Watch your shit." Lorde warned.

"Or what? Huh?" Sage jumped from the truck, ready to square up. She was furious, and wanted to fight this nigga like a bitch out in the streets. "Or what, Lorde?" she got into a fighting stance, instantly.

Oh shit. Lorde thought to himself. He had never seen this side of Sage, and that shit tore at him. He'd never wanted to bring out the ugly inside of her. That shit was whack on his end.

"Together? Ha!" Sage retorted. "Nigga, I've been crying my eyes out thinking that I'm going crazy because I knew my nigga would not step on a bitch toes like that. I've been at constant war with myself thinking I'm motherfucking tripping, but I knew. I KNEW NIGGA! I knew every time you went to see that bitch, because my heart told me so! I hope that pussy was real good, though, because you just lost one!" Sage dropped her arms and backed up before attempting to get inside of her truck.

Before she was all the way in, she felt her neck being squeezed from behind. Rolling her eyes into the top to try and relieved the pain, she turned in her seat. Lorde had the look of death in his eyes as he stared at her with malice dripping from his voice.

"I'm going to get my daughter out of this fucking truck and we're going to go in the house and talk about this shit. You're not going no where. No where. I don't give a fuck about how many times I was with no bitch. All that matters right now is that you've packed your shit talking about leaving a nigga. It ain't going down like that. Not over my dead body!"

"Well lay the fuck down nigga. I'm done with your ass!" Sage barely got out before Lorde had dragged her from the car and onto the ground. His feelings were getting the best of him, and he was willing to do whatever it took to keep Sage at there home.

"Sage, I swear I'll kill you before I let you walk out of my life. This ain't no temporary shit. We forever." Lorde held both of Sage's hands above her head as she wiggled her body on the cold ground.

Sage wasn't interested in conversing. When Lorde allowed her to break free, she was going to show him better than she could ever tell him. Suddenly, Sage broke down under Lorde's spell. He weakened before her, letting her arms go while attempting to console her. Wrong move.

"Sage. I'm sorry. You have to understand that. I fucked up." He demanded that she cheer up. "Please. Just stop crying and come inside so that we can talk about this shit. There's other ways to handle this than you walking out."

When Sage felt comfortable enough, she brought her knee up and lunged it into Lorde's balls. He crunched over, eyes bucking out of his sockets. Sage hurried to her feet, and jumped back into her truck. Lorde regained his composure within seconds, and tried catching up to her. He'd made it to her truck just as the door slammed. Sage didn't even give him as much of a glance before cranking and putting her truck in reverse. As she stepped on the gas, she heard Lorde yell out in pain. She was well aware of the fact that she had ran over his feet –but not one fuck was given. She hoped she'd crushed them bitches so that he couldn't walk into another hoes house as long as he lived.

**

The rays of the sun burned Lorde's forehead even more than the reminders of Sage's absence. She'd left him bruised and burned with a shitload of medical expenses to cover her fit of rage. Lorde cared nothing about the hearty bill. He'd pay it a second time if it meant having Sage return home.

Before his eyes could adjust to the sunlight, he was reaching for his cell. He'd fallen asleep dialing the number that he was waking just to continue dialing. Accessing his recent calls, Lorde tapped Sage's contact, and placed the phone at his ear. Just as last night, he was receiving the voicemail. With little to no hope, he blew out in frustration before tossing his phone on the empty side of the bed.

"Man. Where the fuck are you?" he questioned.

With all of his strength, Lorde lifted himself from the bed to clean his ass and get his day started. Sage was heavy on his mental, but the streets were calling his name. There were people he needed to see and places he needed to go.

Lorde took a shit and bathed to the best of his abilities and was headed for the door. His bald head shook continuously as he traveled down the main hallway, checking out the damages that had been done to the beautiful carpet that Sage had chosen for their home.

"She was on some whole other shit." He hissed.

Lorde locked the house up behind him, praying that Sage would have circled back by the time he made it to lay at night. Although it was wishful thinking, it was very possible. In the near two years since they'd dated, they had never been apart. Lorde was sure that the split would be just as hard on her as it was on him.

The G Wagon was the easiest to maneuver from the drive, so Lorde chose to push it for the day. When he lifted his leg to get inside, a whiff of bleach invaded his nostrils. "UMMM." He backed away from the vehicle. "The fuck?"

After sniffing around for a bit, he realized where the smell was coming from. His carpeting reeked! Upon closer inspection, Lorde realized his floor mats and anything created with fabric had been damaged by the likes of Sage. She'd taken that shit to another level.

"Oh. She really fucking pissed, huh?" Lorde's eyes were wide with surprise.

Lorde used his remotes to unlock each car in the garage. One by one, he checked the insides, and found more of the same. While he wanted to be upset with Sage, he couldn't help but smile. It was the strangest thing, but he was actually happy to see Sage going loco on him. That type of shit made him want to put a ring on her ass. When this was all said and done, he was going to shoot her up with a couple of kids, because any bitch that bleached the Martin deserved to have his babies. That shit was sexy as hell to him.

"What the fuck you standing around cheesing for?" Dade tried blocking the sun with his hand shielding his eyes, but there was no use. He'd popped up on Lorde after calling him all morning without receiving an answer. Sage had even denied his calls. "I've been calling you all morning!" Dade neared Lorde. "What the fuck? What happened to you? Why you ain't call me when them niggas were on your ass?" Dade was foaming at the mouth, staring at Lorde with a patch on his head, a strip over his nose, and a cast on his foot. "Nigga, who…"

"Ain't no niggas did shit, yo. You know me better than that shit."

"Well, what happened?"

Dade looked behind him, and then in front. He was checking the cars for dents or any signs of an accident, but found nothing. He

was in a state of confusion, and needed answers –immediately.
Lorde wasn't talking fast enough, and his bruises weren't adding up.

"Man, Sage got a little upset and…"

"A little?" Dade held his tongue to keep from laughing.
There was no way that he was going to believe that Sage had done
all of that shit to Lorde. He was sounding like one of those women
who swore their face hit the cabinet and not their man's fist. "Lorde.
Come on, B. Sage?"

"Yes nigga! Sage. Don't underestimate my baby, man."

"Aw shit." Dade fell over onto the door of the G Wagon, but
raised up as the smell of bleached attacked him. "What the fuck is
that I smell?"

"My nigga, she went in on my shit." Lorde lowered his head
with a smile polished across his face. "Baby was on the go last
night."

"On go? Nigga you just sitting here cheesing and she done
bleached all your fucking seats. I never took you to be a pussy, dog!"
Dade threw his hands in the air. "The fuck you going to do?"

"Nothing. She found out I was fucking around and lost it.
Ain't shit I wouldn't have done if I hadn't caught her. Only

difference is, there would've been one less nigga breathing on this fucking earth."

Lorde figured it was no big deal. He felt that Sage was justified in her actions. She could've burned the damn cars and house up if it would've replaced the act of her leaving. That shit hurt worse than anything that she'd done that night.

"I feel you on that one." Dade agreed, thinking of SaeKu. "But damn!" he found comedy in the situation. "She fucked you up!" His pearly white teeth gleamed in the sun as he clowned his brother for the shit that his girl had done. Lorde nodded his head, loving the look on Dade's face, and how quickly it was about to change.

"But I wasn't the only one getting my creep on. SaeKu was locked lips with the nigga ass I beat. Jax. Yeah. That's who fucking on her, now. You laughing when you need to be suiting up. Matter of fact, you owe me for beating that niggas ass like I was you! Hadn't I, then I wouldn't be in this shit right now. I could've gotten away, my nigga."

Dade's demeanor changed, completely. His cheeks flushed red, and the hairs on the back of his neck stood at attention. "Fuck did you just say?" Dade questioned, trying to be sure that he heard right.

"You heard me ole prissy ass nigga. Jax fucking your baby mama." Lorde didn't mention another word before Dade had turned around and was high-tailing out of the driveway. Now, it was Lorde's turn to –and he did, *hysterically*.

Chapter Six

SaeKu tiptoed around Dade like a baby taking it's first steps. She'd conveniently been off of work since the day before the big blow up with Lorde. Fortunately for her, she was able to keep a low profile in order to save both she and Dade the difficult time. They'd communicated through text, with her denying his FaceTime calls for, "Dido."

"You're going to have to answer for him soon," Sage chuckled, rubbing Dido's back as she fell asleep across her leg. Sage had been hemmed up inside of SaeKu's apartment for the better part of her departure.

She and Pryce had an amazing suite that was unoccupied. Sage wasn't quite ready to be alone, but she was willing to give SaeKu her space if need be. The two had spent their time together, managing the children and bashing the niggas that they had them with. It was a complete FUCK DADE AND LORDE fest going on at the crib, and no one else was invited.

Sage had blocked Lorde's calls, and even found herself blocking niggas phones that he'd randomly used to track her down. Now, she gave up answering from numbers that she didn't know all together.

"Well, I'll just keep denying them shits until he can't take it anymore."

"That won't be long at all."

"I swear, niggas go crazy when you move on. How long did he expect me to lay at his feet, Sage?"

"Right. I, personally, don't think you've moved on, but Jax is a cute little distraction. I'm just glad you're showing him what's possible, because it is very much so possible that you can grow the strength to roll on his ass."

"Jax is just... I like him, don't get me wrong. In fact..." SaeKu smiled. "I like him a whole lot. I really do."

"But Dade is still floating around in that head and has total control of that heart. It's written all of your face, SaeKu. But, don't let that nigga see that. I say keep liking Jax until that shit transforms into something more meaningful. Show that nigga that his shit does stink." Sage flared her nostrils thinking of Dade. "I tell you about these Livingston men."

"Right. Plus, Lorde made it obvious that I probably shouldn't be dealing with him. I mean, you should've seen the way he was handling him." SaeKu sighed. "Here his ass go, texting again." After a few seconds, she looked over at Sage. "Can you do me a solid one?"

"It depends." She joked.

"Take Dido to Dade in the morning. He's threatening to come through if I don't bring her by noon. I was taking her tomorrow evening, anyway. I have work the next morning."

"Girl, no problem. You know I will. Pryce and I will be getting settled in the room tomorrow. It's about time I faced this shit head on. Lorde hasn't seen her in a week, and I have to arrange some shit with him, too." Sage rolled her eyes at the thought of him.

"You are welcomed to stay."

"No. I insist. Girl, I've been cramping your space. I need to just learn to deal with this shit on my own."

"Like I said, you are welcomed to stay." SaeKu reiterated.

**

"Aye." Lorde rammed his shoulder into Dade's shoulder.

"What nigga?"

"She answering for you?"

"Na, but that's aight. I'm popping up about mine." Dade suggested. "Maybe you should do the same."

"See, I be on that rah rah ass shit with Sage, and she reject a nigga. I figured I should take a different route with this one."

"A different route, huh?"

"Yeah!"

"Well, what the fuck do you consider a different route, because I see you just downloaded the sideline app. That's to switch up ya digits. You about to call her from a different number, AGAIN. I wouldn't say that it was the sanest thing to do, Lorde."

"I'm a hoe ain't it for this shit?"

"Sounds about right." Dade smirked, nodding his head. Lorde sounded like a wounded animal.

"I don't even give a fuck. I'm a hoe and I know it, but I'll be a hoe for my bitch. I miss her shit talking ass. I ain't even been to that discolored ass house since she left."

"She bleached the crib, too?" Lorde asked, covering his mouth with his right hand.

"Fuck you!" Lorde hissed. "And fuck that crib. I got us a new one, already. I had been looking at the bitch, but wanted the okay from Sage. Now, I might as well just gone start moving our shit in that bitch. It's about to be official. I need her to sign off on the paperwork, though. A nigga can't put that shit in his name."

"She must've been pissed for real."

"Yeah. Next time she might cut off my balls, so I'd better chill the fuck out or be more low key with my shit. Honestly, though, I've been thinking. I'm a grown ass man out here in these streets. The only thing I can give a how is a wet ass."

"And that shit ain't worth your family, dog. Temporary pleasure could never amount to a lifetime of stability, support, balance, understanding, nurture, and unconditional love. That's what you get from home, Lorde. After a while, these hoes just become bodies. Everyone starts to look and feel the same. Ain't nothing special about these bitches out here, their chasing a check just like the next, and I ain't got nothing for em, son."

Lorde nodded, taking Dade's words into consideration. "I couldn't have said that shit better. If this wasn't nothing else, it was a teaching lesson for me. I can't even fix my fingers to dial up another bitch right now. That means it was never about them. It was just being locked down and having to sneak around that gave me the thrill. Crazy ass shit, but it's the truth."

"It's the allurement of the game. The fact that you can get caught at any moment keeps your adrenaline pumping. Each time you don't, you up the ante. The risks are higher. The game gets more interesting."

"Exactly. Now, I have no desire to play that shit."

"Ah. What's SaeKu's number?"

"Why?"

"I'm going to put it into the little dialer shit. Sage will think it's her calling."

"Man, you on some real stalker shit." Dade laughed before calling out SaeKu's cell number. Lorde had it stored in his phone, but didn't feel like accessing it.

Lorde connected the call on his cell, and received an answer on the third ring. "You left your wallet. How do you plan on paying for pizza?"

Her voice was as radiant as the bright sun that beamed on Lorde's forehead. He was quiet for a moment, taking in the fact that he was hearing her speak after so many days had elapsed. Lorde couldn't remember missing anyone other than his mother as much as he missed Sage. He needed her to return to him, and soon.

"Hello?"

"Don't hang up." Lorde spoke next, finding his words after a long pause.

"Lorde. What is it?"

Sage sighed on the other end, surprisingly relieved to hear Lorde's voice. As much as she thought she wanted to outcast him, she knew that she couldn't. He'd hurt her feelings, and she could barely think straight. He'd compromised her views and visions for them –shattered the glass house she'd build around them.

"How is she?" he spoke of Pryce.

"She's fine." Sage's voice saddened.

She wished she could reach out and touch Lorde's face, or even hug his neck. Over the year, he'd toughened her so much so that she barely recognized herself. No longer did she want to be macho and mighty. Sage wanted to return to her gentle nature. She wanted to be the mush that Lorde had fallen for, and not the monster that he'd created.

"And you?"

"I'm just me, Lorde."

"It's been a minute. I want to see her, Sage. I want to see you, too!"

"I know. I understand that Lorde. Seeing me isn't an option, but you can see baby girl."

"How are we going to do this? I prefer you just come back home. Sage, I would hate to get stupid and drag you back to the house. You're upset and I get it. But damn."

"Don't insult me! Please! How dare you brush that off like I'm upset for nothing?" Sage's nostrils flared. "Lorde, you're one inconsiderate asshole!"

"Sage, calm down. I know I fucked up and you have every reason to be pissed or do whatever it is that you decide to do… But leaving… that's a little extreme." Lorde calmed down, himself. He was slowly realizing that Sage was ready for whatever, and the strong arm tactic wasn't going to get him what he wanted. She had him by the balls, and he hated that shit.

"Extreme? More extreme than sticking your dick inside of another bitch. Tell me, Lorde. Which would you rather? … Huh? Me leave or allow another nigga to caress the walls of this pussy until my eyes roll into the back of my head and I cover his dick with my cum?" Sage was petty as they came, but she needed Lorde to understand that he wasn't exempt, and the shit could just as well happen to him.

"HELLO?" Sage didn't hear a mumbling word on the other end of the phone, so she figured she'd gotten her point across.

Seconds more would pass before she realized Lorde had ended the call. Rolling her eyes into the top of her head, Sage fell backwards onto the couch. Just as she threw her phone beside her, SaeKu walked back inside of the condo to retrieve her wallet.

"Come on Pryce, put your little arm in here!" Sage smiled, notably. It seemed like an eternity had passed since the last time she had done so. After her brush with Lorde on the phone two days prior, she was finally agreeing to let him see Pryce. "Your father will be here soon."

There was no need in keeping their location a secret. Lorde had connections all around, and their cover could be blown with one phone call. Besides, Sage wasn't in the business of hiding shit. Lorde knew she was not for the games that he wanted to play. She'd waged war, and would square up with the nigga if it came to it. He'd fucked up by creating a fearless being within her, because she didn't even fear him. She respected him to the fullest, but that shit had run low the night she found out about his infidelities.

"I need you dressed and ready by the time this heathen knocks at the door." As the words fell from Sage's mouth, there was a thunderous knock at the hotel room door. "SEE!" she slid Pryce's arm in the other side of her shirt, and swooped her up on her hip.

"Whoah mommy." Pryce smiled, showing the few teeth that she had grown. She was the splitting image of her mother, adorable as they came. Gia had at least done something right by birthing a pretty young girl.

"Woah baby." Sage laughed. She twirled in circles on the way to the door, causing laughter to erupt from Pryce's lungs. "Whoah. Whoah." She kept repeating.

Sage checked the peep hole before pulling the door all the way open. She was certain that it was Lorde, but wanted to check just in case. When she opened the door, he was standing with his hand wrapped around his neck. Sage had to admit that he looked amazingly clad in the denim ensemble of choice. The royal blue shirt that he wore under his denim jacket complimented his… patches.

Sage held her laughter as she examined Lorde's frame. He seemed to have a patch in every place open space on his body. He was even rocking a boot on his foot. It was weird that she wanted to kiss all of his boo boos and dig her fingers in them at the same time.

Hell, she was even willing to give him a few more if it would help her feel better.

"Here." Sage stretched her arms, handing Pryce to Lorde.

Instead of grabbing her, he moved aside, and used the opportunity to get inside of their hotel room. "Really, Lorde?" Sage yelled. "We agreed that you would come get here. What the hell are you doing?"

"You agreed. I ain't say shit. I knew what was up."

"And what's up?"

"We need to talk."

"Na. No we don't. You need to leave before I call security!"

"Sage. Come sit down. I'm not even on no greasy shit, ma. Just here me out!"

"Lorde, I really don't have time for this shit. For real."

"Sage."

"Lorde!" Sage stood at the door with it standing wide open.

Lorde lifted one eyebrow while keeping his eyes trained on Sage. She was a damn fool if she thought he was going anywhere without at least saying what he'd come to say. He knew it was petty to use Pryce to get in her space, but that was the risk he was willing to take.

"Sage." He shrugged. "I've got all night."

Huffing, Sage slammed the door to the suite, and leaned against the back of it. Pryce was making a fuss in her arms, attempting to get down so she allowed her to. Immediately, Pryce ran over to her father and tried to climb into his lap. Lorde had made a seat of the first chair available.

"Da Da. Me miss you." Pryce grabbed Lorde's bald head and kissed the top. "Boo boo?" she pointed at the bandage that was still on his head. The rest of the burns were healing up nicely, but he had to keep that one covered to block out the sun and to keep it from being infected by outside sources.

"Yes, Pryce." Lorde looked to Sage. "Daddy has a few boo boos." Sage lowered her head, staring down at her feet.

"You love me?" Lorde asked.

Pryce nodded her head and hugged Lorde's neck, again. "I love you, too!" he squeezed her upper back, pulling her closer to him. He'd missed his baby girl like crazy, and needed Sage to quit playing and bring her back to the crib. She was on some bullshit, and Lorde was ready for it to be over.

"How long is this going to last?"

"Forever." Sage looked up, finally. "I think it's crazy how you're trying to put a damn time limit on my heartbreak."

"I'm not. I'm not expecting you NOT to feel some type of way, but why you ain't stay at the house and put me out? Y'all living out of a fucking hotel and shit."

"You're honestly acting like it's no big deal."

"It is, though. I promise you it is. I just don't know how I'm supposed to be acting. I told you once before that everything is new to me. I cheat and throw my bitches money to heal the pain. I doubt if them bitches were ever really heartbroken. This…" Lorde looked around. "This is next level shit. I don't know how to respond. What am I supposed to do?"

"I don't know Lorde. There's not much you can do but let me be. I'm so tired of being tough and trying to conform to your standards and what you're used to. I'm just not that girl."

"You don't have to be. I fell in love with you because you were none of the above. I ain't trying to make you out to be nobody that you aren't."

"But you have!"

"That was never my intentions."

"Maybe it wasn't but your expectations have made me rise to the occasion, and I'm not up for this anymore. I'm a fucking softy, a mush, a lover, a girly-girl or whatever name you chose to call it. I wear my heart on my sleeves. I cry when I'm hurt, and I pout when I'm upset. The shit that you did to me broke my entire heart, leaving me nothing to work with, and you are just expecting me to act like this is just a phase. No Lorde. It's not. It's fucking reality!"

Sage yelled. "I'm not the girl you want me to be, and it's best that we both just call this shit for what it is. You reverted back to what you know and what you love. I could never amount to that, Lorde. You're going to get the same thing from me every time. I don't flip flop or change directions every five minutes. I'm the same today and tomorrow. You like chaos. You dwell in dysfunction. It's who you are! It's what you're made of. That's not my world, and I refuse to get sucked up in the the thought that it has to become my world. I don't belong over there. I'm good over here on my side –the less complicated and mellow side." Sage warned. "Just leave."

"Na. I let you talk, so hear me out."

"Fuck you!" Sage spat. "You don't get a turn. Get out!" Sage rushed towards Lorde, making him jump up with the quickness. She had put him through hell a week prior, and he had no intentions of going back. This time, he wanted to be prepared for her foolishness.

"See what I'm saying. That shit gets you off, huh? I bet it does. You thought I was coming on some stupid shit. You have yet to say one thing about all the shit I did to the house and the cars and I can bet my bottom dollar it's because shit like that makes your dick stand. Huh? You like the fact that I got crazy for a minute, huh? Well, news flash. I am not that girl, and you will never take me back to that place. That's why we can't function as a unit. You have issues that I ain't willing to press past. Give me my fucking baby, and get out!"

"Your baby?" Lorde yelled, incredulously. His feelings and ego had been bruised with Sage's words. "We both know you pushing it with that shit. Matter of fact pack MY daughter's shit up.

Got her held up in this piece of shit hotel like she's yours…"

"What did you just say?" Sage's heart thumped out of her

chest. She was sure that she'd heard him wrong.

"Get MY daughter's shit… Matter of fact." Lorde sucked his

teeth. "Don't even worry about it. She straight."

"Lorde, how could you… why would you ever…" Sage's

beautiful skin twisted with confusion. She'd sworn that Lorde had

broken her spirits with his cheating ways, but his words had taken

her breath. The room seemed to spin as she found the nearest piece

of furniture to hold her ground. She'd weakened at his words.

Seeing the effect that his verbal abuse had on Sage, Lorde

closed his eyes and prayed that he could recant. "Man look. I'm

about to be out, just…" he tried handing Pryce to Sage, both girls

crying by now. Sage held her arm out to stop Lorde from coming

any closer to her.

"No. You're right." She nodded. "You're right. She's all

yours." Sage's chest caved as she recited the words. "She's all

yours."

With the little strength that she could muster, Sage found the dresser that held Pryce's clothing, mostly new. She and SaeKu had taken the girls on a shopping trip a few days prior. She begin to remove Pryce's belongings piece by piece. Once her hands were full, she dumped everything onto the bed and then pulled the suitcase from under it.

"Sage, I'm sorry, aight. I didn't mean that shit. I promise. I'm just in a fucked up situation right now. Your words did a nigga dirty, and getting back at you wasn't the right thing to do. Please, forgive me for that shit. I didn't mean it. Sage, she's yours. You've raised her from a jit. I'm so fucking sorry. SHIT!" Lorde cursed, upset that he just couldn't get it right. "I'm fucking up. I'm fucking up big time." Lorde paced the floor, afraid of what was even going through Sage's head. Pryce was a mess in his arms. He rocked her as he walked, attempting to calm her. After a second, she settled.

The clicking of the suitcase stirred Lorde from his daze. "Sage, come on down. I said I ain't mean that shit."

"But you're right, Lorde." Sage shrugged, face drenched. "I have no earthly rights to that little girl. Yeah, I love her and she loves me, but she's yours. I can't keep you from taking her with you."

"But she can stay."

"It doesn't work like that. I'm not going to let you throw up the fact that she isn't mine every time we decide to have an argument, and I'm not going to let you use her as a crutch in this either. You were dead fucking wrong." Sage gritted, placing emphasis behind her words. "Dead wrong, Lorde. Dead wrong. You're really starting to show me your true colors. But thank you." Sage rolled the suitcase to the door.

"Sage. We really need to talk about this shit. You know that slipped."

"Twice, right? Because that should've never even crossed the threshold of your teeth the first time. In fact, it should've never even been a thought. You're even worse than her." Sage retorted, referring to Gia. "Oh my God." Her emotions were running rapid, and she couldn't control them.

"FUCK!" Lorde yelled, scaring Pryce. She whined, touching Sage's heart.

"Goodbye Lorde." Sage wanted to reach out and comfort Pryce, but didn't. she held her hands at each side of her face and watched in horror as she cried.

"Sage. Talk to me." Lorde's voice cracked. "I'm fucking begging you. I ain't meant for none of this shit to happen. I trust that you know this."

"Goodbye Lorde."

"Sage you don't want this shit to end. Don't even act like you do."

"Goodbye Lorde."

Seeing as though Sage was firm in her words, Lorde dropped his head. His hand found the suitcase, and he pulled it behind him. As he walked pass Sage, she reached out to Pryce. "Shhhhh. It's okay." She consoled her. "You're fine. Everything is fine, okay?" Pryce nodded her head, allowing Sage to wipe her tears. "Momma will see you later, okay. Go play with Daddy. Okay."

"Otay." Pryce's body rattled as she spoke as of result of her crying.

"Good girl!" Sage leaned in and kissed Pryce's forehead. "Call me, okay."

"Otay mama."

"Me love you." Sage kissed her cheek, holding it a bit longer than usual.

"Me love you." Pryce made out the best she could.

After shutting the door behind Lorde and Pryce, Sage crippled, sliding to the floor. Her world had come crashing, and she didn't know where to begin to pick it up. She wasn't even sure if she could. Instead of even thinking about it, she just laid –on the floor, surrounding by her own tears.

**

There was no mistaking the masculine figure that hovered over, breathing down Sage's spine. A very lite sleeper, her body stiffened underneath. Her eyes opened wide, surveying the darkness of the hotel room. Before her mouth could express her thoughts, a slight moan escaped instead.

"Ummmmm." Sage chastised herself after realizing she'd showered, and gotten back into bed in all of her naked glory.

Lorde's tongue slid up the crack of her ass, stopping at the lining of her pussy. With his right hand, he lifted Sage from underneath. He didn't have to try hard, because she was assisting. From behind, he sucked her pussy as if it was the sweetest melon that he'd ever encountered.

"Ahhh." Sage moaned like the wounded. Pain mixes with undeniable pleasure had her floating on thin air. "Ahhhhhhhhh."

Lorde received her blessing, and continued on his mission.

"I'm sorry." He spoke. "Sorry for everything." He wanted forgiveness, and he spelled it out on her pussy. Twirling and dipping, he fucked her with his tongue. Lorde wasn't sure if it was the status of their relationship or the healthy foods that she consumed, but one of the two had his mouth salivating from her goodness. Using his left hand, Lorde inserted two fingers, replacing his tongue. He was aiming for the jugular with his violent thrusting. Lorde was no stranger to Sage's weaknesses. He knew her body inside out. He'd probed, poked, inspected, tested, and tasted inch by inch.

As expected, Sage's body was thrown into a fit of convulsions, bring her downward onto his tongue even more. As she sat on his face, she started to rain. Lorde sipped every drop, afraid to waste any of the tasty fluids that she produced.

"I'm cummmmmmmming." Sage called out. "Oh shit." She panted. "Oh shit."

With ease, Lorde lifted his body and slid his pants to the base of his ass. Right under his cheeks, his jeans snugged. His long member massaged the opening of Sage's pussy, elongating her climax. She came for what felt like hours, but was only seconds in reality. Once down from her high, Lorde made promises to help her return.

Sliding into Sage felt better than selling his first ounce of coke. That shit was pure smack. A low growl rumbled from deep within, signaling appreciation for keeping that shit on lock. Sage's pussy invited Lorde in with little to no resistance. Before the split, they fucked a minimum of once a day, which was why Sage couldn't understand why he found the need elsewhere. She made sure to top him off or give him some sloppy pussy before he ventured off into the streets. She gave him no reason to roam, but he'd done so anyway.

"Throw that shit back." Lorde insisted, catching a hip with each of his hands.

He wanted Sage to get her rocks off again before he exploded, because it was coming faster than he'd anticipated. He'd been built up for over a week, now. This first nut would be the quickest. Round two would put her ass to sleep, though.

Abiding by his demands, Sage shoved her ass into Lorde, over and over. Her slimy insides stained his dick as she developed a steady pace. Her eyes were at the top of her lids while she performed as if it was the last show of her life. Sage hadn't realized how much she'd missed the dick until it was back inside of her. Now, she was wondering how she would recover after the slip.

"Oh shit. I'm cumming." The words fell from her lips, causing Lorde to take control.

Grabbing her by the waist, he picked up the pace, pounding into her from behind. Loud smacking could be heard in the distance as he sent her above and beyond. Sage cried out as she climaxed for the second time in less than five minutes.

"Shit. You about to make me nut. Shit. Shit. Shit." Lorde loosened his grip, feeling Sage's pussy contract. That shit sent him up in flames, causing him to explode right afterwards. "Come get in the shower. This shit gone be a while."

Lorde slapped Sage on the ass after they were both able to catch their breaths. Complying, Sage trailed him into the bathroom for a second round. By morning, she woke to an empty bed, and was surprisingly thankful that she had.

Chapter Seven

"Hey." SaeKu spoke when Dade opened the door to his home. "Is she dressed and ready?" She asked, referring to their daughter.

"She ain't here." He informed SaeKu as she stepped through the door.

"What do you mean she isn't here?" SaeKu shrieked.

"I mean she isn't here!"

"Sage came to get her earlier for me. I had a run to make." Dade was less than cordial with SaeKu.

Feeling the tension, she used the opportunity to make her exit. She'd been, somewhat, avoiding the likes of Dade since Jax had come into her life. Lorde seeing them out hadn't made things much better. They had a good little thing going on, and she wanted to see just how far things could go. As she moved closer to the door, she spotted a gold bangle on the table, a shook her head. Dade never ceased to amaze her. Every time she came over, it was some evidence laying around.

"You know you've got me fucked up, right?" Dade questioned from behind.

Not bothering to turn around, again, SaeKu continued towards the door. She knew exactly where this conversation was going, and she wanted no parts. Dade was so unpredictable, and she was tired of fighting with him. At this point, there was not use, anyway.

"You make me strap up my Nike boots and chase your ass down, only to freely give yourself to another man." His words cut like knives, leaving SaeKu no choice but to address them.

Speed walking, she backtracked and got into Dade's personal space. "Don't you dare. Don't you dare blame me for moving on from a man who has barely even noticed me for the last sixteen to eighteen months of my life. One who merely thinks of me as good enough to have carried and delivered his child. One who has made it clear that I am nothing to him and he wants nothing to do with me. One who I craved more than I care to admit to, even, myself some days until I realized that craving would never be satisfied. One who claimed to have been waiting for me, but was as cowardly as they came, sticking his raw dick into a woman and having her birth his first child. One who ripped my heart out of my chest and fed it to the vultures for lunch." SaeKu's finger was unsteady as she held it in Dade's face. "Don't you dare do that to me, Dade."

Unwilling to restrain himself any longer, Dade tugged at her arm. He removed her finger from his face, and forced both of her arms at her sides. His feet begin to move, and before she could protest, he had backed her into the wall next to the door.

"Don…"

Smashing his lips into hers, Dade demanded that she respond by opening her mouth to invite him inside. As he fondled with her lips, his hands roamed over her body, removing her coat from her arms. Her wet tears could be felt on his cheeks as she tried to convince herself that she was above the shameful act that the two were about to commit.

"Dade. No. I won't let you do this to me." She pleaded. "You don't love me. You don't want me. You don't even fucking care about me."

"You know that shit isn't true, and I never want to hear it come from your lips, again." he whispered in her ear.

With his left hand, he rubbed the crotch of her uniform pants. He thought that there was no better sight than to see SaeKu fresh from work with her uniform hugging her newest curves. The navy blue fabric was steaming hot from the heat that emitted from her body.

"I love you, girl, but you did a nigga dirty."

"I said that I was sorry."

"Sorry wasn't going to cut it."

"What do you want from me?" she questioned. "What is it?" Her face was flushed with tears as Dade started back at her, both broken and confused, too.

"I want you to fight for me like I fought for you." Dade pointed into her chest. "You owe me that."

"But…"

"You don't fight to keep what you didn't fight to get, and that's why you let this thing between us go so easily. I was willing to work for it. If I can forgive your fuck up, then you should be able to forgive me for mine. No one is perfect, SaeKu. That's not the world that we're living in."

"But it hurts. It hurts so bad." The pain had yet to subside.

Even after seventeen months, SaeKu still hadn't come to terms with Daicee being Dade's child. She was nearing the eighteen-month mark, and would soon be two. Yet, SaeKu had only seen her four times, and Dade rarely had her on the days that SaeKu was picking up or dropping off. She figured it was his way of keeping the confusion to a minimum.

Dade didn't want to respond to her truth. They had yet to cross that bridge, and his daughter was almost two. Instead of a reply, SaeKu received another kiss –followed by another one. Pretty soon, Dade had her entire body burning with desire. At his front door, he stripped his baby mama of that uniform that he loved to see her in, bent her over, and ran his massive hard up and down her pussy.

As expected, she was wet as a faucet, pussy dripping, and he hadn't even done shit to it, yet. Dade ran his eyes over SaeKu's curves, becoming acquainted with the new additions. He admired them as he readied himself for the thrill that SaeKu was sure to take him on.

"Put it in." she begged, watching him from behind.

His elongated member was hot against her fleshly middle. The thickness covered the width of her vagina, enticing her with every movement. By the way she was acting, one could tell that she hadn't been fucked, but Dade wasn't too sure.

"Put it in?" Dade teased.

"Yes. Please." SaeKu nodded.

Obeying her orders, Dade spread her ass cheeks and allowed his bone to find it's way home. It was no surprise that he had to go through hell to break SaeKu's barriers. He felt a sense of peace having realized she'd been keeping to herself since the split. Upon contact, Dade remained motionless as he inherited the high that only SaeKu could supply.

"Ahhhhh." SaeKu moaned, completely satisfied in that moment.

If they did nothing else, then she'd be happy with the few inches that she'd received. The small insertion was enough to hold her over into the next lifetime. SaeKu didn't crave sex like the normal twenty some odd year old did –unless Dade was in the picture. Now that she had the most magnificent pipe in all history tugging at her walls, she wondered if she would ever recover after a slip of her addiction.

"Damn, girl."

Dade hissed, barely wanting to move a muscle. After what felt like eternity, he was where he'd belonged all along. The tens of women that had seen his sheets over the last year were merely bodies to help him pass from one stage of his horrid breakup to another.

Breaking through barriers proved to be a difficult task, causing Dade to pull backwards, and then forward again. he repeated the same movement over four times before he hit home base. The minute he made the touchdown, SaeKu's limbs became weak. Her

body convulsed, giving Dade the task of maintaining her weight

during the duration of their sexual encounter.

"Ummmmmm." SaeKu had no control over the soulful

moaning that insisted on being heard. As Dade slid in and out of her

slimy pot, her eyes rolled backwards into her head.

While Dade wanted to put his Mac down on SaeKu, and

show her who the fuck he was, he couldn't help but to admire her

growth since the birth of their daughter –both mentally and

physically. He'd done everything under the sun to try and break her

spirits, but she fought him off like plague.

As Dade continued to drill, he marveled over the three stripes

that aligned SaeKu's left side. He had never noticed them before,

meaning they'd appeared as a result of carrying their child.

Squeezing his eyes together, Dade tried not to focus on the painful

reminder of his absence during SaeKu's pregnancy. Her calls went

unanswered, and her presence was unwanted.

Until the day that she went into labor, Dade wanted

absolutely nothing to do with SaeKu. She'd scorn his manhood. Her actions had turned him against her, until he was no longer able to stand the distance that he'd wedged between them.

Once Dido made her entrance into the world, she was his source of contact. She was his ticket back into SaeKu's life. Through his daughter, he was able to have complete access to SaeKu's life. As of lately, that had changed, and he was beginning to feel the affects more than ever. If he had to admit it, he would be ashamed to say that it was driving him insane.

Picking up speed, Dade reached forward and arched SaeKu's back by pulling her hair. Sinking his teeth into her neck, he mumbled he words that he'd been wanting to say for months on end.

"I fucking love you," he groaned, coming to terms with the fact that it would never change.

No matter how difficult he tried being, it would not erase the love that he had for SaeKu. He wanted to hate her for what she'd nearly done, but time had healed his wounds. Now, he was searching for a way to reenter her life without his neglect hanging low over his head. Dade knew that it was too much to ask after all that he'd done to SaeKu, but he wanted a chance.

"Ahhhh." SaeKu was fond of the pleasure, but Dade was near drawing blood. She was relieved when her skin was released from between his teeth.

"You my bitch." Dade didn't have a clue where the words came from, but the thought of another nigga having access to what was his had ticked him off in a matter of seconds. "You think that nigga gone fuck you like this?" he questioned, dipping low while hammering her from behind.

SaeKu didn't care much about what Dade was saying. Her pussy was singing, and hitting higher notes than she'd ever imagined. The euphoric feeling washed over her as he continued.

"Niggas kill about their bitch. You hear me?"

"Ahhhhhhhhhh." Finally reaching her climax, SaeKu clutched thin air, hoping for something to hold onto.

"I'm cumming." Dade announced, immediately after. SaeKu's attempt at dropping to her knees fell miserably as her head nearly detached from her body. Dade wasn't letting her move a muscle as he gripped her tresses even tighter. "Here it comes."

Swallowing her words of disapproval, SaeKu closed her eyes and continued to ride her wave as Dade sprayed his seeds into her oasis. Leaning forward, he kissed her back and neck while breathing onto her skin. Chills raised as SaeKu became engulfed in the skin to skin contact that she was experiencing with Dade. But within a matter of seconds, regret filled the room.

The sun kissed SaeKu's face as she batted her eyes. Sleep had come easy the previous night, and she wished that the nights to follow would be much more of the same. Little toes were the first to be recognized once SaeKu's sight adjusted to the light. *Dido*, she thought to herself. A smile tugged at the corners of her mouth. SaeKu was up in a flash to shower her baby girl with love.

Disappointment quilted her face at the realization that her baby girl was still sound asleep. Running her hand through her messy top, SaeKu sighed. Yesterday had been one to remember. SaeKu eyes roamed the room for traces of her daughter's father, but he was nowhere in sight. As expected, she woke in her own space. Rolling her eyes into the ceiling, she was upset that she'd even allowed herself to slip into his web.

Falling back onto the pillow, SaeKu found herself within a daze, replaying the events in her head once again. It had been well over a year since she and Dade had been physical, and everything about the encounter felt so damn good. She'd be lying if she said that she hadn't once fantasized about such moments, but those hopes and wishes had subsided months prior.

Chiming loudly, SaeKu's cell dragged her from her thoughts. Only a few inches away, she was able to reach over and grab it with ease. Conviction wore heavy on her heart as she read the name sprawled across the screen of her cell.

Jax was calling. SaeKu wasn't exactly sure how to handle the call. On one hand, she really liked him, but on the other Dade's words rang loud in her ear. She was torn between a rock and a hard place. If she wanted Jax to continue breathing, then it was best that she put an end to their time together. Dade had done everything but crawl into her head and embed the fact that he'd murk any nigga that came close to her.

Deciding to ignore the call instead, SaeKu turned to greet her daughter, who was stirring in her sleep. "Hey mamas!" SaeKu swooped down, and pulled Dido into her arms. She had, yet, to even open her eyes. "Mama missed you, Dido!" she sang in her ear, kissing her cheek.

Dido's cried poured into the atmosphere, startling SaeKu. It was the same thing every time. Dido woke acting like she'd been deprived of milk for months. She was the greediest little human SaeKu had ever met.

"Here. Here. Here." SaeKu cooed. She pulled down the left strap to her tee and exposed her breast. Although her eyes remained closed, she was able to locate her mother's nipple. Latching on immediately, Dido quieted down. Finally, she welcomed the sun by opening her eyes. SaeKu's smile brightened as Dido stared back up at her with a frown on her face.

"It's okay little meanie." SaeKu chuckled. "You have your milk, now. Are you happy?" she tickled Dido's nose. Looking down at her blessing, SaeKu was filled with unspeakable joy.

The sound of her phone chirping pulled her from her trance. SaeKu reached over and grabbed her cell without breaking contact with Dido. It was Jax, again. this time, he'd sent a text message.

Jax: Hit me up when you get a chance.

Sighing, SaeKu contemplated texting back, but ended up letting the notification roll off of her chest. Another alert came through, but this time it was Sage. SaeKu had meant to call her when she got up, but she wasn't expecting to sleep so late.

Sage: I'm so threw with that damn Lorde. Remind me to tell you about the hoe shit he pulled with Pryce when he made it here that day.

I just can't believe this shit. She sent a second message.

Bitch ass. The he had the nerve to double back. Just foul. That was the third.

You sure you don't want to come over and talk about it.

Sage: No, I'm not ready to talk about that yet. Did Dade send your baby back in one piece. I was going to bring her by this morning, but he insisted.

Yeah. He brought her here and left her. I guess she was asleep. I swear, I don't even know how that man gets keys and shit. It's scary.

Sage: Exactly. Reason I didn't even give a shit about giving Lorde the deets on the hotel. If he wanted to, he could be up in this bitch. They are the worst type of niggas to fuck with.

I agree with you on that one.

SaeKu continued to breastfeed as she messaged back and forth. As if everyone required her attention at once, her cell started to ring.

"Yeah, Dade?" she answered.

"Trying to make sure you were up. Baby girl gets up around this hour. I brought her by this morning while you were sleeping. I had some plays to make this morning."

"Yeah. I've got her."

"She up?"

"Just got up." Neither Dade or SaeKu mentioned the unsolicited acts they'd participated in the day prior.

"Pick up!"

"Dade, no. I…"

A FaceTime call was coming through before she could say much more. Shaking her head, she connected the call, aware that Dade would keep at it until she did. His handsome face appeared on the phone after a few seconds.

"Dade, we're kind of busy right now. I'm feeding her."

"So, the fuck that's supposed to mean?" he questioned. "Let me see here."

"Dade. Some privacy, please?"

"SaeKu. Stop bullshitting and let me see my daughter."

SaeKu rolled her eyes before turning the camera to face Dido. "What's up mamas?" Dade cooed. Dido, immediately, dropped SaeKu's nipple from her mouth and began to smile. SaeKu pulled her shirt up just as quick, and held the phone in place. Dido had milk leaking from the side of her mouth while she watched her father make funny faces. The two were a match made in heaven, and

SaeKu couldn't imagine partnering with another person on earth to parent with.

"What you doing, mamas? You full? You tummy full mamas?" he laughed. Dido and Daicee were rewarded the same reaction. They were Dade's world, SaeKu included. Although they were apart, she was still near and dear to his heart. "You full, Dido? That baby sleep good last night?" Dade was going to town with the questions as if she could respond.

While SaeKu played the field, she kept a watchful eye out for Dade's surroundings. It was crazy, but she felt possessive in some way. He'd put it down the night before, taking her for three rounds. At this point, she'd be acting a plum fool just like Sage if it meant keeping that nigga's dick in his pants. No bitch deserved dick that good, but her.

"Alright Dade. I'm going to hang up, now." SaeKu warned.

"Aight. When do you go back in?"

"Two days." SaeKu informed.

"Aight. I'll be ready for her."

"Bye."

SaeKu ended the call before pulling her shirt back down. Dido was attempting, but to no avail. Staring down at the screen of her cell, she wanted to text Dade just to break the ice that had been stored around them. To be quite honest, she wouldn't have minded spending one of her days off with he and Dido, but she knew that was asking too much.

Although he stated that he didn't want her seeing another man, he never mentioned fulfilling the gaping hole that had been left since their split. This thing was so frustrating, but SaeKu knew that the only way to get through it was to allow time to bring forth answers. Soon, she'd see whatever light she was searching for at the end of the tunnel.

Chapter Eight

Seven and a half weeks dreadfully passed by as everyone attempted to adjust to the new deck of cards that they'd all been dealt. SaeKu dragged her feet to the doorstep, attempted to turn around and go home for a quick nap. However, she missed her baby girl, dearly. Dade had been providing care for her since two days prior.

SaeKu tapped the door and waited for an answer. A minute of two later, Dade was pulling it open and inviting her inside. He marveled over her beauty in the fitted blue uniform, wishing that he could lend a helping hand. For the last past week, SaeKu had been appearing at his doorstep looking even worn out than each time before.

"You good?" Dade questioned her well-being.

As he went to shut the door, SaeKu noticed a red mark on the side of his neck. The thought of how the obvious hickey had gotten there made her flesh crawl. Every time she showed up to his place, there was another piece of evidence to prove his whorish ways. SaeKu was plain sick of it, and even more upset at the fact that she felt like she had no right to confront him about his extra-curriculum activities.

"Ummm hmmmm. Where's my baby?"

"She's right in here. Come sit down or something, shit." Dade mugged, pulling SaeKu by the arm. She wanted to smack his fucking hand down, but she resisted.

"You don't have to drag me. I can walk."

"SaeKu, you and this attitude can get to stepping. You've been acting like a bitch for the last month or so. I ain't on that shit, yo. Chill."

Nigga, you fucked me and ain't even mentioned the shit. Not to mention all of these hoes you've probably got high tailing through this bitch. Damn right I have an attitude. SaeKu wanted to express, but kept her thoughts bottled inside.

"Whatever Dade. It's been a rough few weeks for me at work." SaeKu tried to downplay her sassiness.

"Yeah. Aight." He nodded. "You hungry?"

"I'll find something in the fridge. I'm ready to get home and lay down."

"SaeKu, you could always go catch up on sleep in my bed. You kill me with this Superwoman shit. You act like I'm not here, alive and willing. Just say the word, and I will take little mama off of your hands for as long as you want. We in this shit together."

"I'm fine Dade. Like I said, work has been demanding."

Sighing, Dade realized he wouldn't get through to her. "Aight. I tried, yo." He shrugged.

SaeKu stood in place while Dade walked into the other room. He returned with a sleeping Dido. He had her bundled up and ready to go. SaeKu smiled, stepping on her tip toes to kiss her baby's face.

"I'm going to put her in the car. You sure you don't want to take a load off, and just skate out in the morning? I'll keep my distance. I have extra rooms if you don't want mine. But, no one goes in my shit. I wouldn't offer the space if they did." SaeKu thought long and hard about her decision.

"And you won't bother me?"

"You have my word."

"And you will keep Dido through the night."

"She'll be wherever I am!" Dade assured her.

"The offer sounds tempting. I'm tired as shit." SaeKu chuckled.

"I can tell." Dade noted. "It's aight to say so, SaeKu. People do get tired every once in a while. You're running yourself thin with work and raising this little girl right here. We ain't got to be exclusive for me to see to it that you're straight. That's my job. Always will be. Now, go chose yourself a bed, and get in it."

Stubbornly, SaeKu headed up the stairs of Dade's home. It was so beautifully decorated. Looking back down the steps, she locked eyes with him. His nod caused her to continue forward. Once inside of his bedroom, her room of choice, SaeKu prepared for bed. She showered, and threw one of his large tees over her head.

She was out before her head could even touch the pillow. The next morning, SaeKu woke up in foreign territory. After gathering her thoughts, she realized she'd slept over at Dade's. Selfishly, she frowned at the empty space next to her. She'd half expected Dade to at least acknowledge some type of connection between the two. Even if it was just simply sneaking in to lay beside her, that would've given her the least bit of hope.

Blowing out in frustration, SaeKu became ill at the thought of how complex the situation was that she was in. On one end, she wanted nothing to do with Dade, but the better part of her wanted everything to do with him. Flipping the covers back, SaeKu stretched before sliding out of bed. She redressed and made the bed, then found her way back downstairs.

Frozen in place, she wanted to back peddle into the room at the sound of Dade's laughter. However, the words to follow his sexy ass comical grumble was saucy. His charm returned as he spoke into what SaeKu guessed to be his cell.

"Say that shit when I see you. I swear you're going to have to back up every syllable of that." There was a pause. "Ah, that's how you feeling?" he continued. "And don't forget that little thing I like."

SaeKu tried backing into the room, but Dade was upon her, now. His face turned ghostly, as he snatched his cell from his ear. He had no clue that SaeKu had waken, and even gotten dressed. Without another word, he ended the call, blindly, and acknowledged her presence.

"Good morning, SaeKu." He smiled, uneasily.

"That little thing that you like?" SaeKu squinted her eyes. "HA! Good morning Dade."

Dade wasn't sure how he was supposed to respond to SaeKu's statement, so he didn't. "I made breakfast." He stated instead.

"Ummm hmmmm. I'm leaving. Where's Dido?"

"She's downstairs. You sure you don't want to grab something to go?"

"I'm fine. I overslept, and need to get a move on it." SaeKu lied. She wasn't sure how much longer she could control her feelings. She wanted to call Dade out on his shit, make love to him, and then live happily ever after. However, it wasn't that simple. It never was with them.

"SaeKu." Dade blew out a heated breath.

"Yeah, Dade?" she turned to face her love and baby's father.

"You sure you don't want none of that shit?"

"I'm sure. Thanks for offering. Oh… and thanks for offering your bed for the night."

"It's nothing." Dade shrugged.

SaeKu found Dido stuffing her mouth with Gerber snacks. As always, SaeKu kissed her face all over before scooping her up. "Let's go mamas."

The two prepared to leave while Dade watched on. He assisted SaeKu with getting Dido into the car, and the two were on their way within minutes. After seeing them off, Dade picked up his cell to call Rachel back. SaeKu had his dick on solid all night, but he respected her space as promised, and stayed to himself. Now, he needed to get his shit off. Rachel knew just how to handle that, with her deep ass throat and bomb ass pussy.

"You ready to eat this dick?" was the first words from Dade's mouth.

**

Sage was finally set on the decision of not returning to the relationship that she and Lorde had created. In her heart, she felt that this would just be the first of many heartbreaks that he would be responsible for. Since their last sexual encounter, she had avoided him at all costs.

"Does these go or stay?" Bella held up the pair of designer pumps with fur trimming the strap that crossed her foot at the top.

"Definitely goes!" SaeKu answered the question for Sage.

They were all gathered at the home that she'd once shared with Lorde. SaeKu was able to get dibs on his location through Dade and had called Sage up to inform her that he would be out of the city for the next 48 hours. Sage had been searching for the perfect window to collect her belongings from the house, and this was her only chance.

Bella had just gotten to town the night before, claiming to need space from her children and husband. According to her, she was spending one more day in the city and would return home the following. Luckily for SaeKu, she was taking Dido with her to see KinZu, her aunt.

"Figured." Bella placed the box on the side that consisted of items that she wanted to take to her new place. Bella had insisted that she call the condo that she and RahMeek owned her own until she found somewhere more suitable.

"What about this, y'all? You think I should keep it?" Sage held up a champagne colored gown with sequin sleeves.

"I love that!" Bella admired the fashionable piece.

"Yes. Keep that!" SaeKu nodded.

"Cool. I have it in black, too. That color just does something for me, though."

"So, SaeKu, what's going on with you and Dade?"

"I mean, nothing. Nothing more than what's been going on. The usual."

"Y'all two just can't even see it, huh?" Bella questioned, posting her hand on her hip.

"See what?"

"That this shit doesn't get easier. It gets tougher. The longer you guys wait to make it happen, the more time you're losing and can't get back. Life is too precious to live unhappily. You stop fucking with a nigga just because he felt some type of way about him. I don't know about you, but if I was not fucking with Meek... he couldn't tell me who had permission to stick their dick in me. If I wanted to fuck his daddy, then that was my business." Bella shrugged.

"It's complicated." SaeKu sighed.

"Not as complicated as you're making it. I mean, really... What's the issue? Don't say the baby, because you still feeling the nigga after that –so that's not the issue. News flash."

Taking a seat on the sofa, SaeKu sighed. "I don't fucking know. I'm just waiting for him to make the first move."

"So, you're willing to wait forever, huh? This isn't hide and seek. You guys aren't at recess. It's either you're going to suck this shit up and handle your business or watch every bitch he knows slide up and down that pole that you seem to love so much that you can't stay off of. Sage, am I crazy is does this bitch clearly look to be sporting a bump?" Bella turned to Sage.

"What?" SaeKu screamed, "You're seeing shit."

Her nerves were rattled, instantly. She'd tried to restrict the thought of pregnancy for the past week and a half. Her cycle had been missed long ago, and she was still in denial of the facts. SaeKu wanted so badly for the odds not to be stacked against her. Another unplanned pregnancy was just too much to even consider at this point in her life.

"Look at her, ready to lie. How long has it been, SaeKu?"

"What do you mean?"

"Since the last time you were sliding up and down that thang? From the looks of it, it was good. You couldn't get off, huh?" Sage joked, calling her friend out.

"This is no laughing matter!" SaeKu pouted. "How the fuck does this keep happening to me?" SaeKu covered her eyes with her hands, and fell back onto the sofa.

"It's happening just the way it is supposed to, SaeKu. You can't stop the inevitable. What's meant will be. You can run and hide all that you want to, but this is God's way of telling you that your plan is not his. How long can you really run from this man?" Bella questioned.

"I'm tired of running, Bella. I just don't know where we go from here."

"You've hit rock bottom. Where else is there to go but up?"

"So wait… You knew that you were pregnant?"

"Not exactly." SaeKu hissed. "I've been kind of just not thinking about it. Oh God. I've been miserably sick."

"Honey. I can spot a pregnant woman from a mile away. I swear. I was wondering which one of you it was. I couldn't quite tell until I paid closer attention to miss thicker than a snicker." Bella laughed.

"Bella. Please. Stop joking about this!" SaeKu groaned.

"Why you looking like someone just stole your best friend. There are far worse things than pregnancy floating around. You'd better be happy that it's only another baby that he's given you."

"She's right!" Sage agreed.

"I know. I just wasn't ready for this."

"SaeKu, some shit we will just never be ready for. Life comes at us fast, and the least we can do is attempt to adjust. This child wasn't conceived just because. In my opinion, this is a token of love. This is your chance to start anew. I know that you want this thing with Dade to work, and here is your proof. You have to put all of the negative thoughts about what went wrong, because that shit is history. If you didn't want the man, he would've never found his way back to that hot ass pussy of yours. Stop depriving yourself, and get your man back. It doesn't matter who says what first. You have a second kid on the way. There is no turning back. That nigga practically owns you, now. You may as well go make amends with your master.

Chapter  Nine

With Bella's words sitting heavy on her heart, SaeKu pushed the door to her SUV. As it collided with the frame, she ironed out the wrinkles of her pressed white blouse. Looking down, she self-consciously, wondered if her small bump was visible. Chalking her thoughts up to the guilt that plagued her, SaeKu inhaled deeply before staring up at Dade's home.

"Well. Here goes nothing." She situated her designer bag on her shoulder, and gripped the handle of her overnight bag to secure it in her right hand.

SaeKu's nerves grew as she neared the door. *Maybe I should have called.* She thought. *He's probably not even here.* She shrugged, seconds away from turning to leave. *No, just get this over with.* SaeKu was battling with herself, afraid to leave and stay. *Just knock on the door.*

Exhaling, SaeKu nodded her head as she gave herself the will needed to continue. Once at the door, she lifted her left hand to knock.

Boom. Boom. Boom.

The loud thuds sounded like grenades letting loose during the silence of the night. Her dark knuckles collided with the wooden frame just before pulling them backwards. *Okay, maybe that was too hard. Yeah. I should just go.* SaeKu turned on her heels, and prepared to leave when she heard the locks of Dade's front door being turned. She chastised herself, knowing that there was no turning back, now. *Oh well.*

"Uh." She squeezed her fingers together before rubbing them on the side of her legs.

"SaeKu." Dade was stunned to see her at his home, unannounced. Not that she wasn't welcomed, but it was not often that she even considered coming by to pick up or drop off their daughter.

Hormones raging, SaeKu was at a loss of words staring back at her baby father, for the second time around. He was barely clothed, in only a towel and white tee shirt. As SaeKu searched for the words to say, her bladder failed her. Pushing past Dade, she dropped her overnight bag and purse at the front door.

"SaeKu, wait." He tried stopping her, but she had taken off.

Tucked away in the guest bathroom that was under the staircase, SaeKu yanked her panties from her ass, and sat to relieve her bladder. Sighing, her eyes rolled into the back of her head while the pressure subsided.

Finally finishing up by tossing the paper towel she's used to wash her hands with into the trash, SaeKu pulled the bathroom door open. She walked back into the front of the house to find Dade dressed in basketball shorts, now. He wore a look of concern as he watched SaeKu near him.

"I'm fine. Everything is fine." SaeKu assured him. "I just…" She started. The minute she reached him, her emotions got the best of her. Holding back as much as she could, her speech commenced.

"I'm just tired Dade. I'm tired of the back and forth. I know I messed up when I decided to abort our daughter without even mentioning the pregnancy to you, but I didn't. I didn't go through with it. She's here, and I'm tired of suffering for a decision that I didn't even see through. I'm tired of looking for something within someone when I have it right here with you."

"SaeK…" Dade held his hand in the air, but she continued.

"No. Let me finish. You told me that I should stop running, and this is it. This is me standing my ground. This is me fighting for us just like you said. I listened, and I heard you. You were right. I'm ready, Dade. I'm ready to fight for this thing…" she pointed between the two of them. "There's no one in the world that can sooth my soul the way that you do. There's no one better to…" SaeKu's heartfelt confession was interrupted at the sight of Claudia, dressed scantily as she descended the stairs of Dade's home. SaeKu cut her eyes in her direction momentarily, but then focused back on Dade. Her chest burned with fiery as embarrassment flushed her cheeks.

"Morning," Claudia waved, making her way down.

"Oh wow." She mumbled, clenching her rapidly beating heart. At any given second, she knew that it would fall from her chest. It was as if everything that she touched went to shits, including the relationship that she was craving with every fiber of her existence.

"SaeKu." Dade started.

"It's fine." SaeKu chuckled, holding her hand up at him. "Sorry I didn't call." She bowed her head, focusing on not falling as she made her way to the door. Bending, she picked up her purse along with her overnight bag.

Dade had yet to notice the small blue bag, because he'd been so busy trying to warn SaeKu of Claudia's presence that he hadn't paid much mind. All of a sudden, things clicked for him. Not only had SaeKu come in peace, but she had plans of staying. Immediately filled with an insane appetite to fulfilled whatever wish it was that she had, Dade reached out to SaeKu.

Sliding to the left, she maneuvered away from his reach. Shaking her head, she started to speak, again. "You know Dade, maybe this just isn't…"

"Don't." he dared her to finish her statement.

Not bothering, SaeKu sucked her teeth before yanking his front door open. "SaeKu. Just give me a minute, and we can finish talking about this. You came to stay, so stay."

SaeKu didn't bother to respond, but continued on her way. Her heart was broken, once again. It wasn't the fact that Dade had

Claudia over that was wrecking her nerves. The revelation that she'd found herself in the same predicament not even a year after her daughter had been born was what was eating away at her. Here she was, expecting a second child by a man that she still wasn't in an actual relationship with.

The thought of going through pregnancy all alone, again, caused the waterworks. That wasn't what SaeKu wanted for herself, and neither for her children. The co-parenting was bad enough with Dade making her life a living hell because he felt like it. With two children, if they didn't get it right, then she could kiss her love life goodbye. Dade would damn near own her. Abortion wasn't even an option, so this was what she'd have to look forward to in life – nothingness.

"I'm not letting you leave." Dade yelled behind SaeKu, jogging to catch up to her.

Wiping her face with her free hand, she sped up to put more distance between them. Her attempts failed the minute she reached her truck. As she opened the door, Dade slammed it closed. The smell of fresh body washed tortured SaeKu's nose.

There were more tears to come as she turned to plead with Dade. "Please. I don't want to do this."

"Neither do I." Dade assured her. "I'm saying, you just gave a nigga a whole ass speech about running, and look at this."

"Don't tell me what the fuck I said. Dade. Let's talk about what you said. Huh?"

Dade was silent as he replayed the conversation that they'd made during their sexual encounter. Before dropping off of her radar, he'd promised that she was the only girl that he had on his mental. Fast forward to the present, and Claudia was prancing around his palace like she was his fucking queen.

"Right." SaeKu continued to wipe the tears, but they were too plentiful to catch. "I can't keep..." SaeKu was a ball of emotions. "I can't keep doing this. Just forget that I even came by."

"How?" Dade yelled. "How the fuck am I supposed to forget you reciting to me the words that I've been wanting to hear since the day that Daicee was born? How, SaeKu? Tell me right fucking now, and I swear I'll take that shit and run with it. Tell me how a nigga supposed to forget that the woman that holds his shit in her hands...

heart, dick, and balls…" Dade grabbed his crotch, and then pressed two finger into SaeKu's chest. "Came to at least try to fight for this shit that we have and leaves even more fucked up than she came. Nah." Dade grabbed SaeKu by the face, and stared into her eyes. "This is us, SaeKu. This storm that we've created is coming to an end, and I'm going to make sure of that. A nigga just needed to know that you hadn't tapped out on him."

"I'm done."

"You ain't done until I say that you're done." He squeezed her cheeks harder, causing her teeth to sink into her jaws.

"So stop saying stupid ass shit like you don't know a nigga been missing you… like I ain't been fucked up since the day you walked out of my house… like seeing you go through that shit with Dido by your lonesome ain't weigh heavy on a nigga's heart… like I ain't been dying inside because I can't hold you like I want to or talk to you just because I can… like I ain't been dreading the day that someone else was at the top of your mental…" Dade leaned closer so that SaeKu could feel the emotion behind his words.

"Like knowing another had the opportunity to make you smile ain't damn near knock a nigga to his knees… like a nigga ain't ready to say fuck the world for ya… like a nigga ain't willing to take it all back just to have you back… like I ain't been joanin' for you since you've been gone… like I don't love you more than the air I breath. Tell me, what I got to do to get this shit back?" Dade stepped back, and held his head high. "You laid your shit out, but I fucked up too. I don't even know how to begin to fix my mistakes, so tell me. What you want? Whatever I broke, I'm ready to fix. Name it, ma, and I'm ready and willing." He admitted, folding his hands in front of him. His heartbeat was erratic as he waited for a response… longing for confirmation. For if SaeKu denied him to his face, again, his world would come crashing.

"Dade, I need to get out." Dade closed his eyes, and cussed under his breath. He'd chosen the wrong night to give in to Claudia's late night booty calls. Knowing that he should've followed his first mind and took his ass to sleep. Now, he was paying for it big time.

"She needs to get out." SaeKu took the brief lapse of emotions to reclaim leverage. Yanking her truck door open, she jumped inside. Before she could take off, Dade was beating on her window.

"Open the door, SaeKu." He demanded, not giving a damn how Claudia got out of his driveway. The bitch could roll over the grass for all he cared. "Or this shit is about to get real fucking ignorant out here."

"Move Dade." SaeKu placed her car in reverse after cranking it.

"Aight." Dade nodded, running around her truck, and lifting himself up by her tail end. Within seconds, he was on the roof of her Lexus. "Put the car in park, and get the fuck out!" Dade yelled from above. He was looking like a wild maniac standing on her vehicle.

This nigga is losing it.

"NO!" SaeKu yelled, completely over his antics. She was wishing that she had never decided to take Bella's word and come over.

"I'm not getting down until you get out."

That's okay. SaeKu mumbled to herself, pressing her foot on the gas, and pulling out of Dade's driveway. *Oh, this bitch is crazy!* Dade thought, hurrying to his knees so that he wouldn't fall from the truck.

He shook his head as he watched the houses in his neighborhood pass in a blur as he focused on keeping himself on top of SaeKu's vehicle. As she came to a stop, Dade hissed, thinking of the crazy shit that he was willing to do for love. His rationality had flown out of the window long ago.

The stop sign at the end of Dade's street was his savior. SaeKu's truck was still as he hopped off the side of it, and tucked his right arm into his shirt. Quickly, he struck the window with his covered elbow, shattering the driver side glass.

"AHHHHHHH!" SaeKu screamed, frightened out of her mind.

Reaching inside of the car, Dade unlocked the door, and opened it. He pulled SaeKu from her seat, and shoved her against the back door. His face was hot like lava as his body was set on fire.

"I'm sick of this shit!" Dade grabbed SaeKu by the neck, and slammed her head into the back window. He hadn't meant to be so forceful, but she had his emotions running high.

"I'm tired of chasing you, only for you to run your ass right back to me. This back and forth shit ends today. Listen to this…"

Dade used his shoulder to wipe the evidence of his heartache from his right eye. "You belong to me, and I belong to you. My bitch." He pointed to SaeKu. "Your nigga." He pointed to himself. "It's as simple as that. The shit in between can be figured out later, but this has to stop. The roof of a car, SaeKu. Really?" he grabbed her right hand, forcefully, and dragged her to the opposite side of the truck.

He opened the passenger door, and waved her in. "I don't want to hear shit. Get in!" he demanded. "… And I promise I'm going to break your fucking wrist if you try to open the door while I'm driving. I put this shit on both of my girls." Dade wanted to make sure that SaeKu understood him.

Slamming the door behind him after she'd gotten inside, Dade took a moment to himself. He was in no rush to get inside of the vehicle, knowing that he was acting on impulse at the moment. If SaeKu said the wrong thing, then her ass would be grass.

Stuffing his body into the driver seat, careful not to cut himself from the broken glass, Dade busted a u-turn in the middle of the street. SaeKu tried stealing a glance at Dade's handsome face.

He was upset, and it showed all over. Her eyes found the floor as he shot daggers her way. Seconds after making a u-turn, Dade was pulling up to his home. Thankfully, Claudia had left. He was the first out, and then SaeKu. He rushed to her side, finally realizing how rough he'd been with her.

The first words from his mouth broke the levees, and SaeKu's crying commenced. "I'm sorry for that shit I did." Dade sighed. "I'm just trying here, aight." Closing in on SaeKu, he extended his arms to wrap the around him, but she kept him at a distance with her hand stretched in his direction.

Nauseated, she leaned over to her left side, and grabbed her stomach with her free hand. All of the crying had gotten her a little shaken up, and the results were sickness. She had not been too keen to sickness when pregnant with Dido, but this pregnancy was much different. If she even looked wrong, she was having a puke fest.

The contents of her stomach poured onto the concrete, missing the grass by a few inches. Over and over, she spilled her guts just a few feet shy of her vehicle. Dade took the hint, and begin to rub her back. He knew that all of the arguing and back and forth must have been taking a toll on SaeKu, because it was taking one on him.

"You good?" he questioned once she lifted back up.

Shaking her head, SaeKu admitted that she wasn't. Truthfully, she felt like shit. Lite-headed and dizzy, she rubbed her forehead to dissect the damages. Just as she thought, she was sweating. "I don't feel good."

"Come on. Come lay down."

"No. I'm not laying in your bed. In fact… I don't even want to go back in your house."

"Fuck the house, then." Dade opened the passenger door back up, and helped SaeKu inside. If she didn't want to go into his house, then she didn't have to. He had a damn near abandoned condo that she was welcomed to at any time. "Let me go lock up."

He reclined her seat before making a dash for the house. Within minutes, he was back out with a cold towel, a bottle of water, and a grocery bag just in case SaeKu became sick to the stomach, again. Hopping inside of the car, he reminded himself to take her shit to the shop asap. Leaning over, Dade placed the folded towel over SaeKu's forehead, and handed her the water.

"Drink that shit." He had twisted the cap off, already.

Crumbling the bag in his lap, he pulled out of his driveway – headed for his condo. The ride was silent as the two became lost within their thoughts. Dade glanced over at SaeKu every so often with thoughts lingering in his head. His mind was playing tricks on him as he dabbled with the idea of SaeKu being sick for a more understandable reason.

As he started to pay her more mind, his senses had heightened. She'd nearly knocked him down to get to the restroom when she first came through the door. Her emotions were all over the place. She'd thrown up for what seemed like forever, and the sickness was lingering. Not to mention, he'd been admiring her constant weight gain. He'd chalked it up to her finally being happy. Now, he wasn't so sure.

However, he pushed the idea from his head being that the thought alone killed him. They hadn't been together in a very long time, and the fact alone could be the death of him. A child by another man would be a pill that Dade wasn't sure he could swallow.

"You feeling any better?" Dade returned to SaeKu's side after returning from having her truck serviced. She'd taken the time to nap, and was feeling a little refreshed.

"Yes." SaeKu nodded. "Did you bring food?" the sun had settled, and night was upon the two.

"Yeah. Where's baby girl?" Dade questioned. SaeKu had, yet, to mention her whereabouts.

"Don't get upset, but..."

"But what?" Dade was in defense mode, immediately.

"But KinZu asked for her for four days. Bella is here, and she told me that she can take her back to Philly with her."

"SaeKu."

"Dade, it's only four days. That gives us both a break."

"A break? I don't need no fucking break." Dade boasted.

"But..."

"Two days." He wrapped up the conversation before it even started.

"Three."

"Three, then. Nothing more."

Hissing, SaeKu rolled her eyes. "I don't care about you being upset. You knew not to make that decision without me, anyway."

"You decided on shit when it comes to her without me all of the time."

"Because I know you'll approve. This is another state, SaeKu. Not just for a quick visit, but she's staying overnight. A few nights to be exact."

Knowing Dade was right, she decided to change the subject. "What did you bring?"

"For one, some clothes so that you can shower and get comfortable."

"No one said I was staying."

"What's understood doesn't have to be explained." Dade shrugged, not even bothering to give into her foolishness. "Go jump in the shower, and I will bring your shit up there."

Dade had stopped by Target to grab pajamas, tights, and t-shirts to store for SaeKu. As long as she wanted, they were staying at his condo. Although he was salty about Dido skating out, he did want to show her mother his appreciation while she was gone. Her absence would give him the time he needed to begin to fix things for them. Hopefully, when she returned, they'd be headed in a completely different direction.

Just as SaeKu stepped from the shower, Dade made his presence known. He'd been staked out in the bathroom for the past three minutes. As she stepped onto the plush floor mat, she jumped back –scared out of her mind.

"Don't do that!" She yelled at Dade, who was busy fixed on her midsection. Snatching the towel from the counter, she covered herself up with the quickness.

"You hiding like I've never seen you before. I've seen it… kissed it… licked it… stuck it… caressed it…" Dade shrugged. "And whatever else there is you can think of."

"Screw you, Dade."

"I plan to."

"Can I have my clothes, please."

"Sure." Dade handed her the semi-revealing pajamas that he had picked up.

"Dade. You couldn't find anything better?" SaeKu held up the two piece, one in which was lace at the breast area. The bottom was a pair of shorts.

"I got what I liked. That other shit was boring."

"So wait, all of the pajamas are like this?"

"Na. The rest are just panties and bras. I thought that I would ease this shit on you, though."

"Oh my God. I'm not wearing this. Where is a t-shirt?"

"Man, stop being difficult and put the shit on."

"I swear you bug. Can you give me some privacy?"

"For what?"

"So that I can put on my clothes, Dade. Come on. Stop being like this."

"A nigga just missed you SaeKu. What's the harm in what I'm doing?"

"There isn't any. I just want a little privacy is all."

"Have it your way." Dade threw his hands in the air, and turned to leave. He was well aware of why she wanted him to leave while she dressed. That little pudge in her stomach could not be mistaken.

"Thank you."

"SaeKu. Let me ask you something, though." He turned as he neared the door.

"Yeah. Dade?"

"Did you give that nigga Jax…"

"Never." Before he could finish his question, SaeKu was answering it.

Nodding, he turned to grant SaeKu her wish. There was no doubt in her mind that she was telling the truth. A sense of pride washed over his handsome face. Rubbing his beard, Dade smiled. After all of this time apart, shit may have been looking up for the two.

SaeKu strolled out of the bathroom looking as delectable as Dade had imagined. Flutters formed around his heart as he stared at her in the natural. For over a year, he'd dreamed of being right in this place. A place of truth, where they could both admit to their flaws and overcome them together. He'd dreamt of this place where they were both willing to let their guards down, and give into the overflowing love that they still felt for one another. SaeKu was his Queen, and he was appreciative of her return to the thrown.

"Can I talk to you?" SaeKu asked, easing on the bed beside Dade.

"Of course."

"I really messed up, huh?"

"Yeah." Dade nodded, "But you know that it happens to the best of us, right?"

"I just…" SaeKu stared at the wooden planks on the floor. "I just don't know what I was thinking."

"You weren't."

"But I was.' She admitted. "I wanted to hurt you as bad as you had hurt me."

"But why? You act like that was intentional."

"Dade, can I just tell you how I really feel. I mean… I just want to get some things off of my chest."

"Go ahead, SaeKu. You have the floor. Say whatever you feel. We need this. I hate that it's taken so long for us to express this shit."

"You say that it wasn't intentional, but I can't help but to wonder why you would ever sleep with a woman without protection that wasn't me. Like, I know that we hadn't seen each other... but be honest. Did you honestly think that I would stray away for too long?"

"No." Dade confessed, facing the same floor boards as SaeKu, now. "Everyday that you were away, I felt like I was a day closer to getting you back. Strange, but truthful."

"So why? Why, Dade?"

"I don't know. It was a fucked up thing to do, SaeKu. I just..."

"You what, Dade? Because let me tell you something... I have NEVER slept with a man since you. NEVER. You want to know why?"

"Why?" Dade had a feeling that she had kept to herself during their elapse, and her voicing it only confirmed things for him.

"Because when you know, you just know. I knew that it wasn't a man on this green earth that could compete with the amount of love that you had for me. I loved the way that you loved me even when I couldn't love myself. I just needed time." SaeKu wiped the tears, trying to stay as strong as she possibly could. "I just feel like when there's something as real as what we've got, you never do anything to jeopardize that. You keep saying that I was running, but I wasn't."

SaeKu nearly choked on her words, so she stopped to collect herself. "I was preparing myself. I was getting myself ready for you. You had so much to offer, and I had nothing." She shook her head, tears slamming against the wood on the floor.

"You didn't need anything."

"Yes I did! I felt so small when I was around you and everyone else. Everyone's life was thriving, and here I was plummeting. I had to get myself ready for what we had in store. There was never a doubt in my mind about the possibilities. They were endless. I'm just not the one to sit at the table. I wanted to contribute. I needed to. You can't possibly understand the mental issues that I was facing back then, Dade. I wasn't running from you… I was saving myself. I needed to discover me again, before I could even allow you to find me. I was hiding, and couldn't even find myself. It would have been selfish of me to watch you search in vain."

"Why didn't you say something?"

"How many times did I?" SaeKu chuckled. "You saw what you wanted to see, Dade. You didn't see me, entirely. You saw fragments."

Nodding his head, Dade agreed with her. She was right. He was selfishly in love with her, and wasn't seeing anything but the reservation that she held when it came to them. Her mental or financial state was not reasons he considered as hindrances, but he was wrong.

"I'm sorry."

"A child, though, Dade. It gets no easier. Yes, it's been a year, but it's still…"

"I know, SaeKu. What you want me to do, though? I can't take shit back. That's my seed, and she deserves to be here just as much as anyone else."

"I'm not saying that she doesn't, but that doesn't make what I'm feeling go away."

"You just need to meet her SaeKu. You've been avoiding this for much too long. I've been aiding it, too. You'd love her. She and Dido are so magical, together." Dade pleaded his case. He knew that SaeKu was ashamed, and her pride was holding them both back from happiness. If he could get her to push it to the side, then things would be good on their end.

"I'm not ready."

"When will you be ready?"

"I don't know Dade. You don't understand. What if I was to have a baby by another…"

"Please don't go there, SaeKu. Let's not make this about that."

Sighing, SaeKu allowed defeat to consume her. "I feel like you don't understand. This really eats away at me. I'm not just overreacting." She cried. "It hurts."

"SaeKu," Dade got on his knees in front of her. "I would never downplay your feelings. I know I fucked up. I know. I'm just trying to figure out how I can right my wrongs, aight? Tell me what I can do to help us get through this together. I'm not trying to make you go through this alone."

"I don't know where to start."

"Pictures." Dade thought. "Can we start there?"

SaeKu thought about what he said, and nodded. "Just not tonight."

"Fine. Not tonight." Dade shrugged. "Now, can I get something off of my chest?"

"Yes." SaeKu nodded, wiping her eyes with the back of her arm.

"When you decided that you didn't want to have my child, you peeled back a piece of my manhood. I think that I was more so upset at the fact that I thought you thought that I wasn't good enough to father your child."

"I never thought that." SaeKu frowned.

"I know. I know. The decision had everything to do with you getting back at a nigga, but I wasn't thinking straight then."

"I'm sorry, Dade. I'm sorry that I ever even tried to go through with that."

"And I'm sorry. I watched you from a far, living out your pregnancy through Sage and Lorde. I should've been there. I know that you may forgive me, but the truth is that I will never forgive myself." Dade said, thinking of how second chances seemed to be in his favor. There was no doubt in his mind that SaeKu was about to give him another one.

"You were there for her birth Dade, and you've been there ever since. That's what truly matters."

"See you'd never understand. I wasn't built like that. I'm a man, baby. I let my pride get in the way of one of the most important time periods of my life. That'll never be okay."

"Dade." SaeKu grabbed his face, and rubbed down the side. The softness that were within them touched her soul. She loved this man more than anyone would ever know.

"There's always been things in between us."

"Always."

"What's next?" SaeKu wondered.

"It's not about what's next, SaeKu. It's about how you and I chose to handle it when it comes our way. I want another chance. I want to finally get this thing right. Don't you want this?"

"Yes. I just need a minute to take this all in."

"More time, huh?" Dade sucked his teeth, not liking the answer that he received.

"Dade, don't say it like that."

"I'm saying, SaeKu. How much time does it really take?"

"Dade, we can't just jump back into the swing of things like nothing ever happened."

Calming himself, Dade knew that she was right.

"I'm just saying give me time to adjust. I want to try. In fact, I'm going to try. I just can't adapt right away. It's impossible."

"You're right. I'm just ready for this." Dade sighed, pressing his back against the bed and pulling his knees up.

Removing herself from the bed, she got on the floor with him. "So am I, Dade. It's not going to happen in the matter of a few hours, though. We've aired our feelings out, and that has to count for something. Baby steps."

"Baby steps." He looked up, and smiled.

"Now, can you kiss me? Please. I've been waiting on this for so long. My God." SaeKu pleaded.

The room seemed as if it had been ignited in flames. The fire that erupted between the long lost lovers couldn't be tamed. With his tender kisses, Dade circled SaeKu's clit for what felt like the hundredth time.

"Ah." She arched her back, and grabbed his head. Running her fingers through his curly top, she encouraged him to continue. "Yes. Yes. Yes."

"Ummmmm." He hummed from below. Using his middle and index finger, he penetrated SaeKu's vagina. He wanted to throw the idea of oral satisfaction out of the window after her walls clamped around his fingers.

"I'm cumming." Her vocals were music to his ears as she warned him that she was near her peak. Picking up the speed, Dade increased the insane amount of pleasure that SaeKu had already been feeling.

"Oh shit. Shit. Shit. Oh shit." She tried crouching, but Dade held his ground as she was lifted from her body and into the sky. Howling, she assured him that she was in utter bliss from his lethal head game.

Taking the time, Dade pulled down his basketball shorts. He couldn't bother with getting them all the way off. The way that SaeKu was screaming, she needed more relief before her high had subsided. Within a few milliseconds, he was pushing the head of his warm erection into her slippery vagina. He could still feel her contracting as he entered her haven. SaeKu nearly drove herself up the wall, tearing up from the amount of gratification that she was receiving. She deemed a dick so good as ridiculous.

"Oh my gosh." She found words, and spit them out as Dade began to maneuver. He was spelling his name in her pussy, staking his claim.

"This my shit?" he questioned, waiting for an answer.

SaeKu could only nod. It was good enough as he leaned down and sucked her lips into his mouth. "I'm sorry." Dade recited as he tucked his face between her shoulder and neck. "I'm sorry." He repeated, again. Stroke after stroke, he reiterated the fact that he had wronged her and was sorry because of it.

"I love you." SaeKu's tears soaked the pillow beneath her. She wasn't sure if she was emotional, or if the dick just felt that good. "I love you so much."

"I love you, too."

Dade went all out to please SaeKu in every way that he thought possible. By the time her body had come down from climax, she was snoring like a baby. While listening to her breathing in the dark, Dade couldn't help but to get one last thing off of his chest. Since she'd been laying in his arms, he'd been trailing the lining of her stomach from top to bottom. There wasn't a doubt in his mind that she was expecting. Because of what had happened the last time, Dade wanted to know what her plans were.

"SaeKu." He called.

"Hmmm?" she answered, trying to stay asleep.

"Are you pregnant?" there was no since in beating around the bush.

"What?" she asked. "No." she lied. "Go to sleep Dade."

Nervous and worried about his reaction, SaeKu chose to lie rather than tell the truth. The minute the words flew from her lips, she wanted to take them back. Her eyes shot open, and she stared into the dark. After a few minutes with no response, SaeKu became satisfied with silence. Minutes later, sleep found her, again.

Still posted behind SaeKu, Dade decided to try and catch some sleep eye. Figuring that maybe he was jumping to conclusions, he threw the idea of another child out of the window. Slightly saddened, he sighed and pulled her even further into his embrace. He couldn't remember the last time he'd felt so whole.

The following morning, SaeKu was up bright and early. With her hair pulled back and the bathroom shower and faucet on, she was sprawled out over the seat of the toilet. The last thing she wanted was for Dade to hear her puking. It wasn't that she was trying to hide the pregnancy from him, but with the lie she'd told last night it would be harder to actually relay the news to him. She figured she would just give it some time.

The sound of the door handle being sabotaged caused SaeKu to jerk her head up and look in it's direction. Seconds after, Dade was cruising through as if nothing was wrong. He'd obviously picked the lock, invading SaeKu's privacy, but he didn't give a shit. Tossing the pink and white box on top of the counter, he grabbed a fresh towel and soaked it with cold water.

"Get up, SaeKu." He demanded with an attitude.

Sensing his hostility, SaeKu forced herself to her feet. Dade used the towel to wipe her face and then her mouth. SaeKu refused to look him in the eyes, instead focusing on the box that he'd thrown on the counter. She hadn't noticed his disappearance, but that was probably because she'd jumped from the bed and been in the bathroom for the past forty minutes or so.

"How are you feeling this morning?" he gritted.

"Not so good." SaeKu felt as if there was no reason to cover up what they both knew was the truth.

"I want you to piss on that stick." He dropped his hands to his sides, and stared her in the face.

"There's no use." SaeKu mumbled.

"Excuse me." Dade wanted to be sure that he was hearing her correctly.

"There's no use Dade. I'm pregnant. AGAIN." SaeKu shook her head, and tried maneuvering her way out of the bathroom.

Dade allowed the news to sink in for a few before he reached out to grab her. He could feel the emotions that played into her confession, and he wanted to know why they were so saddened.

"Why'd you lie to me?" he questioned.

"I don't know. I just…"

"Is it mi…"

Reaching back, SaeKu hauled off and slapped the shit out of Dade. Instantly, he could taste blood inside of his mouth. Before he could access the damages, SaeKu had stormed out of his bathroom, and into the bedroom. Still dressed in pajamas, she begin to throw her clothes on over them.

"SaeKu."

Dade became frantic at the thought of her leaving, again. He knew that he was foul for the question he'd asked when they'd had the conversation and she'd expressed that he was the only man she had been with since their first encounter. With every fiber in his being, he knew that to be true. His lips had failed him, and he knew that he had fucked up.

"Fuck. I ain't mean that." He tried reasoning with her.

"Really Dade, because it sure as hell sounded like it." SaeKu continued getting dressed. By now, she only had her shoes to slip on.

"Why are you always running?"

"Na." SaeKu chuckled. "See that's where you're wrong. This isn't me running. This is me being the bigger person and leaving before this shit turns sour."

"SaeKu."

"Obviously, you have some personal issues that you need to be working out. I've never given you a reason to think that I had community pussy. Who do I look like having unprotected sex with a man other than you, Dade? I swear, you just keep on surprising me." SaeKu shook her head, and began to search for her keys.

"I know, SaeKu. That shit just slipped."

"Well, I'm glad to know what you were thinking."

"Man, I'm so sick of this back and forth shit."

"This isn't one of the cases, and I won't let you guilt me into staying when I don't want to. I'm not running, Dade. I meant what I said. I just..." SaeKu shrugged. "You hurt my feelings, aight?" she was upfront and truthful with him.

"I apologize." Dade closed in on SaeKu.

"Well, you know... Apologizing isn't going to take the words back, Dade. I have to go." She told him, finally reaching her keys.

"Go where?"

"Away from you, nigga. I need to get some rest, because I feel like shit. Furthermore, I want to spend this time without my daughter relaxing. We're arguing more than we're making up, and now just isn't the time for that. Every time I yell I feel the urge to puke. This pregnancy is driving me up the wall. I can't let you do the same thing."

"Have your fucking way, SaeKu!" Dade held his hands up in surrender.

He was over the fighting and fussing. As long as she knew that this shit between them was forever, then he didn't give a damn what else she was talking about. Besides, with a new baby on the way, he needed to get a few things situated. Without SaeKu in his hair, he could move freely.

"For what it's worth, I apologize about lying."

Without another word, Dade removed himself from her presence. Both pissed, the two allowed each other some space. SaeKu ventured down the stairs and out of the door. As expected, her truck was looking as good as new. She forced her body inside before cranking and pulling off. The thought of a long hot bath and a day of rest sounded intriguing as she drove home.

Chapter Ten

Night had come before SaeKu was back up from a much needed nap. Food was the first thing on her brain, but her cell rang and interrupted her thoughts. Damn near certain that it was Dade calling, she answered the phone with an attitude. She was still upset about the fact that he'd questioned their child's paternity.

"What Dade?"

"Wait, trouble in paradise. I thought you were going to get your man back?"

"I did." SaeKu yawned. "But, he's back in the dog house."

"What did he do this time?"

"For starters, he had company."

"That's to be expected. He's a single man."

"Over my dead body."

"Now, that's the shit I like to hear." Sage clapped her hands in the background. "Now, what else?"

"I told him I was pregnant."

"…And."

"He asked if it was his!"

"Okay, you acting like you gave the man a reason to believe otherwise. You've been prancing around with Mr. Goodbar like Dade ain't peeped that shit. Y'all fucked what… one time? How do you expect this man to believe that you became pregnant from that one time? You know how niggas think…"

"They don't."

"EXACTLY." Sage yelled. "You get my point."

"Whatever."

"What are you doing?"

"Just woke up. I'm about to be in search of food."

"SaeKu. I can see it now. This baby is going to make you one miserable bitch."

"Fuck you. What do you want, anyway?"

The phone line grew quiet as Sage figured out how to reveal her next set of words.

"Hello?"

"Yeah. I'm here."

"What's wrong?" SaeKu became concerned. She could hear the sadness in Sage's tone.

"I have to stop drinking the water when I come to your house."

"What?"

"It must be something in it."

"Stop playing. What are you talking about?"

"It had me sick for days. Then, I went to the doctor earlier, and they told me that I was 6 weeks pregnant. I could blame no one but you. It's either pregnancy is contagious or it's in the water at your crib. You really need to get that checked out."

"Bullshit!" SaeKu sat up.

"Bullshit!" Sage rolled her eyes into the top of her head. "It's as real as it gets SaeKu, and I don't even know what to do."

"What you mean you don't know. You carry the baby to term, and then you birth it."

"I'm saying... I don't know what to do as far as Lorde. Who knowingly wants to become a single parent, because that's what I'll be?"

"Have you talked to him?"

"No. I blocked him."

"What about Pryce? You people have a child together. How can you just block the man?"

"Because, that's all on him. Do you know that in the heat of the moment, he mentioned me not being Pryce's mother?"

"Lies!" SaeKu wasn't going to believe that.

"I'm serious, SaeKu. That shit hurt me to the core. I promised to leave that man alone after then, and now this."

"Sage, you couldn't have thought it would be that simple. Don't forget you said 6 weeks. Y'all have been split longer than that. You're leaving out a few details."

"He caught me during a weak moment, and I caved." Sage admitted. "I should've never even let that nigga into my space."

"And then you wouldn't be expecting my niece or nephew. Cheer up. At least he's good for something." SaeKu chuckled.

"Right."

"I say call him up, Sage. Just have dinner with him and tell him the truth. After that, just leave it all in God's hands."

"I miss that crazy ass no good ass nigga." Sage sighed.

"Ain't nothing wrong with missing him, Sage. I didn't reveal his infidelities for you to leave him. That was your decision and I was with it no matter what."

"I couldn't stay, SaeKu. He did it dirty after all that shit he's already put me through."

"You're right about that, but does it seem like he's learned anything."

"I mean, when I did speak with him, he sounded down and out."

"Because he's going crazy without you."

"Shit, I'm going crazy without him." She admitted.

"See." SaeKu started. "Maybe it was just that one time."

"I can't be playing with my own damn heart like that."

"You're right, but I know niggas like Lorde. All it takes is one time for you to leave their asses, and they're flying right from then on. RahMeek did the same shit to Bella, and she doesn't even have to be in his presence for him to carry himself like a motherfucker with a wife that will leave his ass in a blink."

"I don't know."

"Just give it some time. Besides that, how are you feeling?"

"I'm fine. Hadn't I gone for my annual, then there's no telling how much longer I would've went without knowing."

"I'm so happy for you!" SaeKu squealed on the other end.

"I need a favor."

"What's that?"

"I have a doctor's appointment tomorrow, and I need you to cover for my assignment."

"Of course." SaeKu agreed. "Send me the itinerary, and make sure to mark me in your spot. You don't have to worry. Go ahead and check on the little one. Schedule a dinner or something while you're at it. Go see your man." SaeKu decided to throw the little hint at the end. She knew that Sage was miserable without Lorde, and prayed that he had gotten his shit together.

"I don't know, SaeKu."

"It has to be done, whether tomorrow or two weeks from now. You and I both know that Lorde is a great father and would want to know just like you do. Don't hold back from him, no matter what y'all are going through. You see where that shit landed me."

"I hear you, SaeKu. I just need to come to terms with this myself."

"Don't you want him to accompany you to the first visit?"

"Not really. I wanted to check things out for myself a bit, first."

"I feel you on that one. I'm not going to one appointment alone this time. If Dade could go in my place, I swear I would let him."

"Well, that understandable. He hid behind Lorde your entire pregnancy trying to find out what was going on. My dumb ass allowed him to trick me, too. That bald headed sucker never mentioned you until after he'd fucked me damn near to sleep. I would tell him anything he needed to know to shut up." Sage chuckled.

"I swear I had no clue. He just mentioned it to me last night. Niggas are wild, man. Pride wouldn't let you step up to the plate, but you're here, now. Crazy."

"Right. I know for a fact he isn't missing this one. He was walking around like a sick puppy the entire time. I bet he cheesing now."

"I don't know why. I'm not talking to that nigga until next week. He blew me with that question."

"You'll be back over there, tonight."

"Watch and see."

"Well, I'm going to send over all the info that you need. I'll give you a call in the morning."

"Okay. I'm about to find something to eat in this kitchen."

After ending their call, SaeKu lifted herself from the bed, and walked towards the bathroom –sluggishly. She emptied her bladder before finding her way into the kitchen. Deciding on tacos, she pulled out the turkey ground beef to unthaw. In the meantime,

SaeKu figured she'd snack on apples and caramel, and catch a movie.

Mid Netflix search, her cell pulled her from focus. Without much thought, she grabbed it and checked the caller's identification. Of course, it was Dade calling. Not in the mood to talk, she pressed ignore and then placed her phone on do not disturb.

Continuing her search, she went through a small serving of apples, and went into the kitchen for more. When she returned, the light of her cell caught her attention. She'd received three additional calls from Dade, and two text messages. He was doing the most. Not bothering with the calls, she checked his messages.

Have you eaten? Was the first. Assuming he'd read her mind, SaeKu rolled her eyes into the top of her head.

Answer the fucking phone. She knew his patience was growing thin, but she cared nothing about his feelings at the moment. He hadn't cared anything about hers.

As she was attempting to exit the messages, the gray bubble appeared and then another text. *You see these messages with your evil ass. Is this what I have to look forward to through this pregnancy?*

A smile threatened SaeKu's lips as she rolled her eyes and threw her phone to the side. She had no time to play Dade's games. She'd answer to him when she was good and ready. For now, she only wanted a movie and some food to fill her stomach.

**

Sage sat idly on the bench and watched the children around her play. She'd come to get some fresh air, and be alone. However, she found herself surrounded by a heap of children who were enjoying the simpler things in life. As she watched the young girl with long pigtails play, tears blurred her vision.

The little girl reminded her so much of herself as a child. Thinking back to better days, she pondered over the death of her parents, and how she would never get to see the joy in her mother's eyes after telling her that she was expecting her grandchild. Sage wondered if her father would approve of she and Lorde's relationship, and furthermore their conceiving out of wedlock. So many thoughts raced through Sage's mind at once that she became lite-headed and short of breath.

Taking her time, she tried gaining her composure. After a few seconds elapsed, she felt her rush come down. Nearly back to normal, she reached into her pocket and retrieved the sheet of ultrasounds that the doctor had allowed her to take home. Staring at the images, she was completely unaware of what she was seeing, but it was beautiful.

Just as she begin to marvel, her phone vibrated in her pocket.

"Hello."

"Sage. I've been trying to get at you for days, yo. Everything good?" Concern was etched in Lorde's voice. Each time they spoke his spirit sounded a bit more defeated. Their separation was hell on the both of them.

"Everything is just fine, Lorde. Is there something that you guys need?" she asked, referring to he and Pryce.

"You." He was honest.

Sighing, Sage wiped the tear that threatened to slip from her face. She knew they needed her, and she needed them as well. "I know, Lorde. I know." She mumbled into the phone. "I just need... I don't know what I need, really. I'm just trying to figure things out."

"Let's figure them out together." He pleaded. "You've got a nigga not even wanting to get out of the bed in the morning. I ain't never felt no shit like this before. What the fuck is going on with me?"

"It's called heartbreak, Lorde. It happens to the best of us."

"Come back."

"I can't do that, Lorde."

"Why'd you even leave? We could've worked this out."

"You left me no option."

"It was one time."

"It would've been two and three had I let it." Sage was becoming frustrated.

"You're missing the point, Sage. I'm not justifying my actions. I'm saying that you could've given me time to correct them."

"Lorde. I have to go." Sage was ready to end their call all of a sudden.

"Pryce and I miss you, Sage. Can you at least stop through or something?"

"Lorde, that's asking too much."

"Please. I'm trying to be civilized because you say that you don't like that crazy ass shit, but what choice do I have right about now. My nigga, I'm growing blue balls because I refuse to fuck anybody that ain't you. I ain't even have no hoes… just that one hoe. That shit was done the day it got exposed, because I knew what the fuck I had at home. I was trying to avoid this, and you still left me. How selfish is that?"

"Really Lorde?"

"Yes! Really. I'm a sorry ass nigga, and I know that. But shit, we been through too much to just say fuck this shit. We have a daughter and all of this shit."

"WE have a daughter?" Sage asked, hissing.

"Damn right. Don't even bring that other shit up, because that don't count. You know that I was talking out the side of my neck on some other shit."

"Well, you said it, Lorde. I don't think that people say shit that they don't mean."

"I did." Lorde sighed. "What's it going to take, Sage? Shit. You giving me gray hairs and I'm bald."

Sage wanted to laugh, but this was a serious matter. All of a sudden, their unborn child came to mind. She knew that she'd have to open up to him soon. There was no need of running from the inevitable.

"I don't know Lorde. You haven't really done anything other than call a few times a day. Begging and pleading is getting you nowhere."

"Well come over and let me fuck. Let's see how far that gets me."

"Bye!" Sage hung up the phone before she actually took him up on his offer. It was tempting, especially with her raging hormones.

Shaking her head, Sage continued to stare out into the open space. An hour passed, and she found herself still in the same place. The bench beside her shifted, and she was filled with a sense of pride as she saw little feet peddling her way. She didn't have to acknowledge the suitor next to her, because the little person that was walking her way occupied every ounce of her attention.

"Mama's baby!" she tried placing the sonogram inside of her purse, but felt it being tugged from her hand.

She didn't object, but gave the roll up freely. Pryce's hair was all over her head, not a bow in sight. Sage wanted to be made at the small bits of visible tangles, but blamed herself for not coming by to comb Pryce's hair. Lorde was like a fish out of water trying to care for her wild tresses.

"Me miss you." Pryce spoke, hugging Sage's neck.

"I missed you, too. Love."

Lorde sat in silence as he gawked at the sonogram in front of him. His eyes went from Sage's name to the small figure in the grayscale photo. His heart beamed with pride and pained at the same time. Not only had he impregnated the love of his life, but he'd fucked her over as well. Without a doubt, he knew that a child wasn't in Sage's plans, and he'd purposely gotten her pregnant on some foolish shit. She was the girl that dreamed of wedding and doing shit the right way.

Disappointment consumed Lorde as he thought of the turmoil he'd brought to this woman's life, and wondered if he was even fit to fuck with her anymore. While he'd felt entitled for the longest, their time a part had him thinking differently. He'd humbled himself, something that he'd only experienced with his mother. Yeah, he loved Sage and wanted her back, but she was just too damned good to him. Lorde could only identify with complexity, and she only had balance to offer.

He was enthralled by the vicious ghetto women, and Sage just simply wanted love. While the drama thrilled Lorde, Sage strayed away from it. Lorde was used to diversity within his women, not knowing what type of bitch he'd wake up to, with Sage it was always clear. He'd wake up to kiss on the forehead –and even breakfast in bed. When he walked through the door, he was sure to be showered with love versus an argument. Even when Sage was gone off on trips, she'd come back the same person that she left –and simply missing her man and child. Not to mention it was a child that she hadn't even birthed.

She was everything that he was not, and it had Lorde feeling some type of way. There hadn't been a woman on this earth that he'd ever felt incompetent with, and then came Sage and her beautiful soul. Tarnished and ill-minded, Lorde was everything but optimistic about the future that he had to offer Sage. What more did he have to offer her other than bullshit?

"How did you find me?" Sage questioned.

"I have my ways." Lorde shrugged.

Nodding, she went on. "I just found out. I've been sitting here for over two hours trying to figure out where my life goes from here, you know."

"It can only go up from here." Lorde stared at the side of her face as he watched her pull a brush from her purse and begin to detangle Pryce's hair. She was so gentle-natured.

"I mean like… having a child was not in my plans, or at least not so soon. I had saw so much more. This was much further down the line." Sage didn't know if she was happy or sad in the current moment. Confusion covered her face. "I guess I'm just feeling a little overwhelmed."

"Is there anything that I can do to help resolve that feeling for you?" Lorde wanted to help make her feel better any way that he could.

"No." she admitted.

"How you feeling about this? Straight up?"

"Sad. Happy. Mad. Joyful." Sage shrugged. "I can't really tell you right now. Ask me later this week and I'll know for sure."

Nodding in understanding, Lorde continued. "I know this isn't a place for this, so what do you say to dinner tomorrow night? I just want to get some shit off of my chest, and you can figure out what you want to do from there. I promise not to push or pull. I'm just asking for you to lend an ear and a bit of your time." To be quite honest, Lorde was out of his element.

His demeanor, conversation, and entire existence screamed defeat. He knew that his mother was rolling over in her grave for the way that Lorde was behaving himself with someone deserving of the world. He'd acted a plum fool since the beginning of their relationship, and was beginning to see that it was not becoming. For the last month, he'd tried stepping back and awarding Sage with her space, hoping she'd come around. Even that had failed, crippling him.

"Dinner sounds like a plan." Sage agreed without hesitation.

"Yo, you serious right now?" Lorde found a bit of his heart in a more upbeat space. A smile tugged at his lips as he waited for an answer.

"Yeah." Sage nodded. "I just feel like we need to talk at some point. The last thing I want to do is stress while carrying. Anything could happen."

"You're right." Lorde agreed. "Pryce, you hear that. I get to have dinner with your mother while you go to your nanny!"

Lorde made a mental note to try and keep Sage's stress levels down, seeing as it was something that she was concerned about. He was mentally thinking of everything that she'd ever complained of, being sure that he didn't revisit the act again. If he was planning to make this thing work, he would have to start by listening.

"Why would you tell her that?" Sage chuckled.

"It's the truth."

"So, that was mean."

"She's a tough kid. She ain't even say nothing back."

"Because I gave her candy. That's the only reason. Can she spend the night with me?"

"Come on, now, Sage. You killing me over here. Why is that even a question? None of this…" Lorde pointed between the three of them. He regretted ever saying those words to Sage. "None of this changes. Don't act like that."

"It was just a question, Lorde."

"A question that put me back in a place of regret. Stop acting like that, Sage. You know you have just as much say over Pryce as I do, or more. That's all you right there." Lorde stressed. "Yo, I'm going to get out of here." He was back in a bitter mood. "Can you take this session to your place?"

"Yeah." Sage grabbed the trinkets that she had pulled from her purse and put them back. "Come on, baby." She lifted, bringing Pryce with her.

"Aight. I'm going to walk y'all to the car."

"Okay."

"Just make sure that you take her to the sitter before you come through. I'll be ready for you around 9."

"Sounds a little late for dinner."

"If it's too late when it's time for you to leave, I will. Like I said, no pushing or pulling."

"Sounds good to me." Lorde had walked them to the car as promised. He assisted them inside, and then turned to leave.

"Sage."

"Yeah."

"I fucked up, but I promise that shit opened my eyes. Give us some thought tonight. If you don't mind, I want to keep these. I can cut you half when you come through. If you can just get over that one thing I did, then I promise you'll never regret another day with me. You're all I've got out here. Ain't nobody about to look out for me like you do. I'm off that shit, Sage. Fuck with a nigga this one time."

"See you later, Lorde." Sage smiled, and closed her car door. For some reason, she knew that what Lorde was saying was true. She felt it in her heart that he'd learned a valuable lesson.

Chapter Eleven

Night had fallen before SaeKu was turning the key to her condo. She'd experienced a fairly complicated workday, and couldn't wait to get a free day at the spa from Sage for accepting it. SaeKu opened her front door, and anxiety shot through her chest. She stared at an empty space, much like the one that she'd witnessed before moving her furniture in. The only difference was that most of her accents and wall décor was still in tact.

"What the fuck?" she questioned. Snatching her phone out of her pocket, she dialed Dade's cell with the quickness.

"Yeah."

"Someone broke into my place." She begin to back out of her condo, afraid of what was waiting for her on the inside.

"I did." Dade admitted.

"What do you mean you did?" she stopped in her tracks.

Without another word, Dade ended the call, and shut off his cell. Taking a peek back inside of her place, SaeKu slowly went inside. Looking around, she took note of everything that Dade had taken. *This nigga has lost his fucking mind!* SaeKu thought. She tried calling him back, but received the voicemail instead.

In the center of her living room was sheet of paper, tucked beneath a key. Bending, SaeKu grabbed both. Heart and face were both on fire as she read the words that Dade had scribbled on the back of an old piece of mail.

This is just what it looks like. I'm done playing games. If we're going to do this, then we're going to do this together. We're expecting our second child, and I refuse to miss another second of it's life playing childish ass games. For now, OUR condo is home. When you free up, I have a few listings that we can swing by and look at. We're going to need more room before the baby gets here. With this letter is a key. Use it. I'd hate to have to come get you. I love you SaeKu.

Baby daddy (second time around)

Rolling her eyes up to the ceiling, SaeKu wondered why he had to be extra and put the last little bit. He didn't have to keep reminding her that he'd managed to knock her up twice within a two-year time span. That fact was well noted.

Twirling the small key inside of her palm, SaeKu sighed before turning to leave, again. Had Dade at least left a bed, she would've considered staying, but he'd taken it all. With one last sweep over her place, SaeKu closed the door and made her way to the car. Twenty minutes would pass before she was pulling under the carport at Dade's place.

SaeKu popped her trunk, and grabbed her suitcase, being that she didn't seem to be going anywhere any time soon. Dade was finally putting his foot down, and she liked it –strangely. Not only had she been forced to fight for their thing, but after years, his fight had yet to die. It made her feel good knowing that he still wanted everything to do with her. Dade was a one of a kind man, and she knew that she'd never find anyone remotely close to his caliber.

All hadn't been forgiven, but nothing was too traumatic for them to try at. That's what mattered the most –they were both putting forth an effort to progress as one. SaeKu's trunk slammed, nearly catching her finger. She snatched her hand backwards before laughing at how clumsy she was. Shaking her head, she took a deep breath before looking up on Dade's balcony. The lights were still on, meaning that he was still up waiting for her return. Shrugging, she figured she'd may as well stop stalling.

The elevator ride was quicker than usual, but SaeKu didn't bother to complain. Her feet were killing her, and the bed was calling her name. The thought of being wrapped inside of Dade's arms was enticing. In just another day, they'd have Dido back, which made matters even better. She'd have both of her favorite people in the same space, for the first time ever.

For the second time in one night, SaeKu was turning the key to a door. After removing the gold piece of matter, she stuffed it inside of her jacket pocket so that she wouldn't lose it. Gabbing her bag, she pushed the door open and walked inside of the condo. She could smell the aroma of food, making her mouth salivate. Sitting her suitcase by the door, she hurried into the kitchen to see what all the fuss was about.

Before she could take one too many steps, Dade appeared, wiping his hands on his pants. The sound of laughter was to follow his trail, causing SaeKu's heart to thud out of her chest. Instantly, her palms became sweaty, and she felt sick all over. Fever rushed her body, consuming her unwillingly. Her mouth became dry all of a sudden, as her eyes followed the sound of a little voice.

"Daddy Dido ride wagon!" the precious sounds of an innocent baby girl raked away at SaeKu's chest.

Before her was a high yellow version of her own daughter, pulling a red wagon behind her. Inside of the wagon, Dido was deeply tucked with her hands in the air and laughter pouring from her vocals.

Hastily, SaeKu back peddled through the door that she'd just come from. While she wanted to be released from the sight before her eyes, she couldn't bring herself to turn away. Using her senses, she felt for the door handle, snatched it open, and backed out of the door. As she made her exit, she managed to trip over her own foot. She fell to the floor, ass first, and was paralyzed, instantly. She couldn't move a muscle, not that she'd tried much either.

Hyperventilating, SaeKu sat on the floor outside of Dade's condo with her heart sitting right next to her. She felt the weight of the world on her shoulders at the moment, trying to rationalize and come to terms with everything that was happening around her.

She hadn't expected to see Dido so soon, and surely not Daicee. SaeKu had made it clear to Dade that this thing would take time, yet he'd gone about this his own way. She felt as if he was shoving this thing down her throat, making the situation worse than it had to be. It would take forever for this thing to work if he continued to disregard her feelings.

"Hey." SaeKu felt Dade reach for he. Although she wanted to snatch away, she was too drained to move. "I'm sorry about that. I should've told you, but I was afraid you wouldn't come."

"We talked about this." SaeKu fought to get out. "Why are you forcing this down my throat Dade? I said that I was going to get through it, but this is no way to go about things."

"It's not what you think, SaeKu. I swear. I didn't do this on purpose."

"How do I know that?" she finally looked at him.

"Because I wouldn't do that to you. Alani was in an accident, and she's messed up pretty bad. I agreed to get Daicee out of the way for a week or two. She looked so damn bored without her sister, so I took the trip to Philly to get baby girl. That's it. That's all. That's how they both ended up here, today. I had already moved your shit out, so there wasn't any going back. This is just what it is right now, SaeKu. I need you to put your big girl panties on and be here for me."

Breathing, hard and labored breathing, was all that was to follow Dade's comment. SaeKu was lost inside of her own bubble for an eternity as they sat in silence. Dade's face contorted, wondering about the thoughts that lingered within her mental space. He wished she'd speak them out loud so that he could intervene, and swing things in a more positive direction –sure that her thoughts weren't of the best caliber at the time.

Forever seemed to pass before Dade received a response. "Help me up."

He didn't mumble another word, but assisted SaeKu like she asked. "I know this is overload right now, but I promise it's all good."

"I know Dade. I'm just having a hard time with this. That's all. I'm ready for this, though. All of this. I didn't expect it to be today, but what can I do, huh?" SaeKu wiped her drenched face and braced herself for what was to come. Taking a deep breath, she continued. "Besides, I'm tired as hell and I couldn't even fathom going to check into a room." She chuckled, making lite of the situation.

"You trying to make a nigga marry you or some shit?" Dade smiled, showing off his pearly whites. He felt like a proud father in that moment. Finally, SaeKu was ready for whatever. That's the type of attitude he'd been waiting for her to obtain since the beginning.

Moving closer, he grabbed her by the neck, and tongued her down. Their tongues danced as they both became engulfed in one another's presence. "Come on." Dade broke away. "Let me feed you and then put you to bed."

"Sounds like a plan to me."

Grabbing SaeKu's hand, Dade led her back into the house where he'd placed the girls inside of the plastic fence that he had tucked away in the closet. Of course, Dido was trying to find her way out.

"Get your daughter!" Dade pointed at their chocolate slice of heaven.

"Hey mama!" SaeKu smiled as she walked over to the play pen where the girls were. She started to reach for Dido, who was excited to see her, but then changed her mind. Lifting her leg, she climbed inside where both of the girls where. If she was going to do this, she was going to do it right.

Dade's mouth nearly fell to the ground as he witnessed Dido and Daicee both crowd SaeKu. One would never know that it was Daicee's first real encounter with her. Stuck in place, he pulled out his cell, and snapped a quick photo. The sound of his camera caught SaeKu's attention, causing her to look his way. The biggest smile spread across her lips as she realized this was exactly what Dade had been yarning for all along. In that moment, she made a vow to grant him the peace and serenity that he was deserving of for the rest of her life.

I love you, she mouthed as she gathered the girls on her lap. She wanted Dade to get the best group photo as he could.

"You sit here, Daicee. Dido. Come back here, girl." Dido was in no mood for sitting still. SaeKu snatched her behind up, and placed her next to Daicee on the other side of her. She put up a fight, making SaeKu shrug her shoulders.

"Bae, this is about as good as it gets."

"It's perfect." Dade snapped away as Dido tried climbing back to the floor. "Come to the table."

Dade tucked his phone away, and made his way back into the kitchen to fix plates. He was on a natural high with the thought of SaeKu and Daicee's union on his mental. This was a night to celebrate. He couldn't wait to get SaeKu alone. He planned to eat that pussy from the front to the back. If he could make it from the bed after their session, he planned to plant the biggest rock on her finger for her to wake up screaming his name, again.

Dinner was filled with laughter and smiles. SaeKu could admit that Daicee was a true character, just like Dido. The two were a match made in heaven. Daicee looked out for her little sister, and could barely look out for herself. Knowing that SaeKu was burnt out from work, he was managing the girls well. It was a joy watching him interact with them so lovingly. SaeKu was approving of the closeness that he'd managed to create between the two. It warmed her heart, causing her to wonder how their sibling would fit into their little posse.

"And soon there will be three." SaeKu sighed.

"I went from none to having three in a heart beat."

"I feel the same way." SaeKu nodded. "Everything happened so fast."

"That's how life works. I prayed for this." Dade admitted. "All of this."

"Even me?"

"Even you." He nodded.

"I prayed for this, too, Dade. I really did." SaeKu bowed her head.

"Don't do that. I know you did."

The tears started, again. "I just feel so stupid. This feels so good, and I've been running from it since the beginning of time."

"SaeKu, don't fault yourself. I had my hand in this shit, too. We had to be pulled apart to get ourselves together. We good, now. Look at you... You handled your shit like a G, tonight."

"I did, huh?" she smiled, wiping her face. "I wish I could stop crying."

"You've got a few more month before you can control that shit."

"Don't even remind me." SaeKu responded.

"How you feeling about the baby, SaeKu?"

Shrugging, she started. "I mean, Dido is my world. I couldn't see pass her at first, but with this pregnancy I can see it clearer. I, honestly, want this to be the last, but I want this one –nevertheless. Plus, I feel like it's both of our peace offerings, our chances to get it right. It's my chance to forgive myself what my thoughts about Dido in the beginning, and for you to forgive yourself for your absence. Not to mention, this little love child was the sign that I asked God for. I had given up on us. It's like, we needed this."

"Everything you just said confirmed everything I'd been thinking about all day. I can't lie, SaeKu. I'm happy as a motherfucker to be witnessing this shit first hand this time. All of my girls are together this time. You and I are where we need to be. Everything is perfect, and we can both enjoy this pregnancy and the rest of our lives together. That's baby number two, so you're officially my old lady." Dade chuckled.

"I already figured as much. That's why I brought my ass on over. I said this is it. I might as well stop trying to run, because I'm never going to get away, now."

"I'm glad that you came to your senses, because I would've been a lunatic hadn't you."

"Trust me, I know."

As promised, Dade fed SaeKu and put her to sleep. The vibration of her cell woke him in the dead of the night. Putting his plan into action, he slipped from the heat of her naked body and stalked over to the closet. Inside, he dug around in his coat pocket before landing on the velvet box that he'd been fondling with for the past two days.

Grabbing it, he opened the case and the most beautiful rock stared him back in the face. SaeKu had never taken off her initial "engagement" ring, and still wore it to remind her of the romance that they shared. He had no intentions of her removing it either. She could just add this piece to the pie.

Sliding back under the covers, he searched through the dark for her fingers. Her left hand wasn't hard to find, with the oversized ring that he'd blessed her with long ago. Increasing the worth of her ring finger, insanely, Dade slid the piece on in the dark. He wasn't expecting SaeKu to agree to marriage the minute she saw the ring. He just couldn't wait another minute to reveal his thoughts, by sharing the precious jewels. When the time was right, they'd both know. If that was tomorrow, then so be it. Next year would even due for Dade. Just as he drew back to take his spot on the pillow next to her, the vibration of her cell commenced –again.

Frustrated, Dade knew that it was no respectable call being made at such an hour. Leaning over SaeKu, he invaded the little privacy that she thought she had by snatching up her cell. Had it been his, he'd expect the same from her. Just like that, whatever boundaries they once had were now broken. Looking at the caller I.D., he sighed when seeing Sage's face cover the phone.

Tapping the green button, he answered, startled by the confession on the other end.

With labored breathing, Sage could barely recite the words, "We need help."

Chapter Twelve

A smile crept upon Sage's face as she waved to the sitter before pulling out of the driveway. She'd run behind on time, but Lorde promised her that all was well. It was past the ten o'clock hour, and wouldn't be in his space until at least halfway through it. Sucking her teeth, she chewed away at her own ass for not setting an alarm to wake her sooner. The nap she had with Pryce has run over by an hour. She woke, disoriented and having the most difficult time finding the swing of things.

Ringing roared over the Bluetooth, startling Sage –whom had forgotten that she'd just dialed a number. "Hello," Lorde's voice connected with the fragments of her tormented heart.

"I'm pulling out. I shall be there shortly."

"See you in a bit." Lorde smiled, ending the call.

He looked around the neatly decorated house, that he'd had a hand in helping to decorate. The bulk of the work had been done professionally. He wanted this night to be perfect. After dinner, he had plans on asking for one more chance at this relationship number with Sage. Although he had an inkling that she would accept, a dark cloud lingered over his spirits.

For the strangest reason, he couldn't shake the feeling of gloom that consumed him. He'd called to check the traps at least three times in the last five hours. All of his soldiers were in place, assuring him that everything was good on their end. Dade was in check, playing the family man that Lorde was desperate to become within the hour, and Sage was on her way to his place.

Shrugging, he looked up to the Lord with a quick prayer in tow. After reciting just a few words, Lorde went into the kitchen to light the candles that littered the neatly decorated table. Letting his guard down, he'd crossed every limit set by the G code that he followed. He didn't give a fuck about none of that shit if it didn't mean having his lady feel special in a time of despair. He needed Sage back more than the druggies needed their next hit. She was his addiction, and the withdrawal symptoms to follow her absence was too much to bare. At this point, Lorde would explore all measures to bring him that high, again.

A knock at the door warned Lorde of Sage's presence. He was puzzled as to why she hadn't used her key. Until she was ready to come back home, Lorde refused to move into their new place. He wanted to grace it with both of their presence. Lorde knew that Sage had went ballistic the night she found out about everything, and could bet that she had tossed it somewhere. It didn't bother him one bit, just as long as she hadn't stood him up.

Lorde walked to the door with a smile on his face. He couldn't wait to see his lover and friend. He'd been so empty without her that it hardly made any since. Her absence caused a huge disruption in his life. That shit had to come to an end, ASAP.

Unhooking the latch and unlocking the door, Lorde could barely get it open before it was pushed in on him. An AK was aimed at his head, and a nigga with a mask over his face had a handgun shoved into Sage's back.

"I'm sorry." She cried. "I knocked." She reminded him of the distress call that they had created. He was so caught up in the mood that he hadn't even notice she knocked three times, and then twice more. He'd given her those instructions in case of an emergency like suck, and instructed her to never use her key. This would give him time to prepare for whatever was on the other side of the door.

"It's okay. Stop cr…" Lorde felt the butt of the gun connect with his skull. "AH shit." He cursed. "What the fuck do you want bitch ass nigga?" he questioned his intruders.

"For you to be in such a compromising position, you sure got a lot of shit to say."

"Jax, my nigga. I would've never thought you had it in you!" Lorde was no bitch, with or without his pistol he was a solid nigga. Bitch was the furthest from his makeup.

Sage's eyes bulged from her sockets at the name. Jax was the guy that SaeKu had been dating. This shit was getting crazier by the second. Sage was aware of the damage Lorde had done to this man, so she knew he was coming to prove a point. Without a doubt, she knew that they were not going to make it out alive.

Jax knew that his cover was blown, so he pulled the hot ass mask from his face.

"Who is this you brought with you?" Lorde questioned. "He knows he's a dead man, too?"

"Go check the house." Jax instructed his partner, and he did just that. While they waited for his return, Lorde tried devising a plan.

Sage was posted beside him, after being pushed to the floor. They both sat by the door, with a gun to their bodies. Lorde tried thinking in the compromising situation, but Sage's whimpers kept causing him to lose his train of thought. Looking to the right of him he shook his head, signaling for her to stop with the tears. She was making it hard for him to concentrate.

"Where the fucking cash at?" Jax questioned.

"Yo, ain't shit in this bitch." Lorde was truthful with his response. He never kept cash around the house. He was well aware of the rule, never shit where you lay.

"Where the fuck the shit at, then?" his partner questioned.

"It ain't here, nigga!" Lorde spat from his mouth.

"Nigga, either you telling us where the fuck it's at or I'm killing your bitch ass!" Jax yelled. "Where the fuck is the cash at?"

"I have some!" Sage cried. "Please. Don't kill us. I have cash."

"Sage!" Lorde gritted. "Don't you…"

"I can show you where it is!"

Sage would do whatever just to save their lives. It was true. She did have cash stored in their house. It was near $10,000 that she kept in the closet of their bedroom in two show boxes. She'd store the money over time from the loose money that Lorde would randomly hand her.

"Sage, where is it?" Lorde questioned. He would take them niggas, but she wasn't going no fucking where.

"Na. She can show me." The wing man shouted down the stairs, and started making his way down.

Lorde was fueling on the inside. He didn't know that nigga, and he didn't trust that nigga. He was ready to blow a fucking gasket watching Sage lift from the floor. With this gun, he pushed her forward and trailed her back up the stairs.

It took everything in Lorde not to get up and go after her. He knew that if he moved, all hell would break loose. He stayed put just to protect his woman and unborn. He couldn't risk their lives on that foolish shit.

Sage hiked the steps, slowly, trying to think of the last place that she had seen Lorde place his gun. He had several, but he was always moving them. Sage had plans of getting the money, but she also had plans of making it out alive. She had a child to live for, so something was going to have to give. She didn't give a fuck how she did it, but she and Lorde needed to make it out safely.

Sage reached the bedroom, where the light was already on. She walked slowly, surveying her surroundings to see what was where –praying to spot the shiny piece of metal. With no luck, she felt a nudge on her back as she was pushed into the closet. She turned towards her aggressor with a smudge look on her face.

"Turn around." he said, a little too creepy for Sage. For some reason, her mind warned her against making the move. She stood firm, not turning as she had been instructed. All of a sudden, her palms were beginning to sweat. Dissecting the situation, she realized that the second intruder had other intentions. He'd succeeded at getting her alone and inside of a closet. Lifting the gun above her head, he brought it down onto her face.

The stiff piece of matter crashed into her frame, causing her to yelp in pain. "Turn around." he assisted her by shoving her body in the opposite direction. He held his gun in his right hand, and controlled her movements with his left. After he had her turned away from him, he placed the gun at the back of her head.

"If you move, I'm shooting you!" he warned.

Sage began to weep, immediately. She was well aware of what was about to happen. "Get to the ground." He demanded. Slowly, she made her way to the plush carpet, afraid to move too fast and be hot in the head.

Unfortunately, Sage was dressed to kill in a wrap-around skirt and fitted shirt. She felt the tip of the gun on climb her leg as the wind blew beneath her skirt, assuring her that it had been moved to the side. She held her breath as she felt heat from her attackers body as he hovered over her.

"Please." Sage began to cry, squirming from beneath. "PLEASE. DON'T!" she yelled.

"Shut up, bitch!" he tried striking Sage with the gun, again, but missed.

Holding her head into the carpet with his left hand, he used the hand that was equipped with his gun to pull his joggers down. His dick stood at attention. Without thinking twice, being that he had little to no time, he lowered himself to Sage's level and held his piece at her ass. He slapped the head on her cheek, pleased to see it jiggle. Sage tried removing her head from the carpet, but there was no use. His firm grip made it impossible.

Without warning, Sage's attacker rammed his penis into her pussy. She yelped in pain, finding enough strength to lift her head, finally. He humped like a wild animal, stretching her beyond belief. The dryness of her vagina made the feeling even more horrid.

From the bottom of the step, Lorde was able to hear the distress call from Sage. Something wasn't right. He didn't think much about his situation, spinning into action immediately. At this point, he was ready to die about his. Motherfuckers would just have to lay him to rest, because he wasn't no hoe ass nigga that could just sit and listen to the cries of his girl and not do shit cause a nigga held a gun to his dome.

Lorde barely lifted his frame before he was jogging up the steps. Jax was right behind him, aiming his pistol at Lorde's dome. With an unsteady aim, he fired his shot, knocking Lorde backwards, and back down the stairs. Jax had put one to his head, ending his shit before he could even reach a hollering Sage.

The single gunshot alarmed Sage's attacker, causing him to drop his own weapon. Sage used the opportunity to grab it before he could. It had fallen just beside her. She'd quickly gained control of the situation, flipping over and firing the gun with her eyes closed. She didn't stop shooting until the clipped had been emptied. When she opened her eyes back up, she was welcomed with gun smoke, and splats of blood all over her upper body.

"Oh my God." She cried, unable to move. "Oh my God."

Her mind was in a frenzy as she looked around at the mess that she had made. The black skull cap was inflated, and Sage was certain that it was brain matter that had caused it to swell. She had riddled her rapist's neck, face, and head with bullets. Sage attempted to lift herself up, but an excruciating pain shot through her abdomen. Her face contorted and she stayed put until the pain subsided. She was unsure of what was going on downstairs, but she knew that she needed to get to a phone. Scooting herself around on the floor, in too much pain to do much else, Sage patted down the dead man before her. He didn't have a phone.

"FUCK!" she cried. Using the thick carpet, she dug her hands through it and used it to help her reach the house phone that sat on the nightstand just feet away. She dialed the first number that came to mind. She would go on to dial the same number two more times before she received an answer from Dade.

Chapter  Thirteen

SaeKu sighed, willing herself to get out of the car as she sat in the lonely parking lot, tears staining her cheeks. In a split second, life as she knew it had been ripped to shreds. Everything around her was, unpleasantly, different. Everything about her world was touch and go at this point. For what seemed like eternity, she'd been living in a miserable pit of hell begging to be freed. There was nothing that no one could do to pull her out, but rescue two people that she cared deeply about, both Lorde and Sage.

The robbery had set the couple back as a whole, stealing nothing materialistic, but claiming the mental and physical state of either. While Lorde was tucked away in a hospital bed, awaiting an awakening, Sage was stuck behind a caged facility, and deemed a nut case.

The thought alone drew tears to SaeKu's eyes, once again. For the life of her, she just couldn't pull herself together. "Just get out." She kept telling herself.

It was the same prep talk that she had alone each day. Since the incident, she'd taken a leave from work, strongly considering ditching the job, completely. Her personal life demanded too much of her, and she wasn't so sure about returning after it's demands were met.

Finally listening to her inner voice, SaeKu latched on to the door handle of her truck before sliding out. Using the back of her sleeve, she removed the traces of tears, but the evidence of an emotional state lingered in her eyes and demeanor. There was no shaking the uneasiness that she was suffering from in general. She was merely making it, and it was notable.

She stalked to the door, and was buzzed in shortly after. The entire smell of the outdated facility gave SaeKu an upset stomach. There was nothing that she managed to find about this place to be appealing, other than the fact that they were keeping great watch over her best friend. However, after the day ended, she wasn't even sure if that would be good enough.

"Ms. Noble. How do you do, today?" Sherry, the receptionist questioned.

"Same as yesterday, and the day before." SaeKu shrugged. Her tone was bland, much like her existence at the time. She was so out of tune that it angered her inside. She'd never been this disconnected with reality. The severity of the situation still jolted her.

"I understand. These things can be difficult. That's a lovely ring you have there."

So much had gone down that SaeKu had yet to thank Dade for the ring that she'd discovered on her finger the day after the fiasco. Everything was so fucked up that she couldn't even think of good enough words to recite to him, so she said nothing instead.

"Thanks."

"She's up." She spoke, training the conversation to Sage.

"Good. Any development?"

"None."

"Thanks Sherry." SaeKu nodded, and headed for Sage's quarter. While guest visits were restricted, SaeKu was an exception of the rules. Dade had made sure of it.

"Sage." SaeKu stood in the door, purse dangling from her arm.

The white suit that fitted loosely on Sage's frame was horrid in SaeKu's eyes. In that moment, she wanted to remove her dear friend from her own insanity, and bring her back to their world —one that giving up or in wasn't an option. However, no matter how hard she tried, Sage just wouldn't return to her. She wouldn't even make contact, always in a very distant space.

As expected, her demand was met with silence. It didn't bother SaeKu as much as the day before, or the day before that. She was slowly coming to grips with Sage's compromised mental state. It was the sole reason she'd kept her in the institution to begin with. With the pregnancy, Lorde's condition, the safety of the children, and caring for Pryce all connected, there was little room to put up much fight for the inevitable.

However, it did nothing to discourage SaeKu. The heavier the load, the stronger the fight, she thought often. This was by far her toughest battle, and she was wearing thin trying to stay in the ring. Focusing her attention on Sage, she stepped deeper into the room, before stretching her arms around her best friend. Nothing had changed, and it never would.

"Hey, Sage. I brought you some things. I'm sure they're trying to feed you shit as usual. That's why you're not eating, but we have to get something inside of the tummy of yours. Can't have you around her deprived. Enough has been taken from you, already." SaeKu was going on and on as she stepped back and went into her purse. She'd brought a few trinkets to get Sage through the remainder of the day, sure that she'd return the next with more.

Silence.

Sage remained quiet, her eyes still lost in a far away place. Her hair was braided in nice cornrolls to the back, thanks to SaeKu, and her skin was pale due to the lack of sunlight. Although she was hiding somewhere inside of herself, Sage's beauty remained undeniable.

"Sage, please." SaeKu begged. "Just talk to me."

With those words, SaeKu rested her head towards the ground, attempting to hold back. The situation she'd been thrust into was no place for an expecting mother. Her emotion were the root of an on coming breakdown, and she just prayed that it didn't lead to serious problems for the health of herself and her child.

Feeling a burning in the side of her face, SaeKu looked up to see Sage staring back at her –something she hadn't been blessed with since the incident. The small gesture caused a collapsing of breath, SaeKu was astound.

"Sage. I know you're in there. Everything is alright out here. Please. Just come back to me." she pleaded, hopeful that Sage was there somewhere.

SaeKu returned the glare, searching for an answer within Sage's big brown eyes. Emptiness and pain appeared through the glossed over balls. SaeKu tried reading the message written within them, but it wasn't legible. At least not to the naked eye. For what seemed to be a lifetime, they stared at one another.

"Please. Pryce needs you." SaeKu mumbled, reaching out to squeeze Sage's left hand.

At the sound of Pryce's existence, SaeKu witnessed the film that covered Sage's eyes submit to her emotions. She was feeling something, SaeKu continued to note the progress. A tear slid down her face, but neither of them moved to catch it. Mainly because another was to follow, and then one more. Three tears, that was all Sage produced, but those three droplets of salty liquid assured SaeKu of many things. One being that Sage was still there, fighting. Although it seemed that way, she hadn't given up. She was resting, and one day she'd return.

No further progress was sowed on Sage's end. In fact, she quickly reverted back to that far away place. After SaeKu spoon fed her, with much resistance, SaeKu packed up and prepared to accompany Dade for a few hours. She was tired, as usual, and planned to get some shut eye if she could.

**

It had been a full three weeks, and much had changed in Lorde's condition, besides the fact that he had yet to wake. Dade sat by his side, idly, each and everyday. He was waiting for a miracle, a wink or blink. He desperately needed a sign that all would be well. Doctors were expecting him to pull through, but Dade was a man of evidence. Until he saw his brother's eyes, then nothing was well in his world.

As the thought occurred, movement commenced in his peripheral. Sure that he was bugging, Dade continued to stroke SaeKu's tresses as she slept peacefully in his lap. She'd been out for less than twenty minutes, after an emotional outburst while speaking of the nature of Sage's condition. She had revealed the progress that she'd made right in front of her eyes, and then how soon she reverted back.

Dade tried to rest her worried bones, but couldn't. After instructing her to lay down, he rubbed her back, neck, face, and hair to calm her. Within minutes, she was out like light. It was, now, Dade's turn to worry about his mans. Just like Sage, his health was a horrid factor that remained on Dade's radar for all of the wrong reasons. He needed him to wake pronto. There was a ticking time bomb walking around with an entire clip with his name sprawled across it. Dade just simply needed to know who he was assigning his bullets to, because some motherfucker was about to get it.

Again, the bed shifted. Even minimal movement was noticeable from a bedside where it was nonexistent. Cocking his head to the side after turning it, Dade waited for another tell tell sign. Seconds would past before he'd be relieved of the breath he was holding. Swiping his leg clean of SaeKu's head, he stood to his feet and rushed to the bed where Lorde was attempting to gain consciousness.

With batting eyelashes, Lorde fought the jagged feeling that had consumed him for way too long. He'd been fighting fatigue for a little more time than he cared to. The familiarity of Dade's voice startled him, shaking him up in the process, but for reasons more clear as the seconds grew into minutes.

"Lorde." Dade called. "Come on." He continued, but there was no use.

Lorde was wide awake, still fighting the urge to go back under. However, he was afraid to acknowledge the absence he'd felt since his arrival in the underworld. Where was she, he questioned in his head. In the earlier half of the hour, he'd heard SaeKu's frustrations with Sage's health, which caused the fight in him to strengthen. Now, minutes later, he wanted answers. He'd waken just to receive them.

"Ah." Lorde tried speaking, still flickering his eyes.

"Wait." Dade held up a finger, dipped into the restroom, and returned with a cup of water. They hadn't kept any in his room due to the fact that he couldn't get up and drink it himself, so there was no use. Dade made due, though.

Pushing the control button on the side of the bed, Dade hit a few before finding the correct one. The bed raised, and Lorde's eyes were wide in shock as he sat midair. Dade placed the cup at his lips, and Lorde opened to receive the water that he was being given. After it was finished, Dade rushed back for more. Three cups would disappear before Lorde shook his head, assuring Dade that he didn't need anymore.

Staring straight ahead, Lorde felt his personal space being compromised. He was so accustomed to being the solid, unfazed, and untouchable that he was struggling with the words needed to be revealed. For, this would declare a deficiency —making him incapable of the one thing that he had neglected to value along with the woman that he loved. It was the simple shit that he had merely thought about, and no wished that he'd appreciated more.

In his most vulnerable state, he tried to focus on the man in front of him, but failed. A devastating blow struck his beating heart, as he prepared to make an unbelievable confession. Soreness crowded him, causing physical and emotional pain. Like a frightened child, his lips began to quiver. The words fell from his lips as if they weren't being forced, but Lorde knew the truth of the matter.

"I…" he started, a lone tear gracing his face. "I can't see."

Dade's entire world shattered in front of him.

Backing away from the bed as if it was plagued, Dade dropped the forth cup that he'd heled to Lorde's lips in an attempt to flee. The plastic matter hitting the floor caused a stir in SaeKu's sleep. She opened her eyes, partially, witnessing her man run for his life. She almost went after him until she noticed Lorde was awake in bed.

"LORDE!" SaeKu rejoiced. "Oh my God."

SaeKu sprang into action, calling the on-hand nurse from the button on the remote to the television. "You're awake." She yelped after ending the call.

"How is she, SaeKu?" the small rasp was still present, but SaeKu could understand him –nonetheless.

"Sage will be fine. It's just taking time. So much happened that night."

"Did she?" Lorde couldn't find the words to ask the question that he'd been dreading the answer to. "Did she?"

Before SaeKu could respond, the nurse had rushed inside to Lorde's aid. "She did." SaeKu thought out loud, causing an unexpected reaction within Lorde. For the first time ever, she saw his state weaken.

An unmistakable groan left his lips as he covered his face. SaeKu didn't have to be a rocket scientist to determine when a man was hurting. His disposition was striking as his back heaved in and out. He was definitely crying. Lorde was crying. Really crying.

SaeKu hadn't recognized the wetness of her own cheeks until the nurse handed her a hand full of Kleenex. She'd been frozen in place, witnessing a father baring the thought of losing his unborn child. The rape had caused Sage to miscarry, which was another reason she'd slipped into a world of her own.

SaeKu could no longer stand to see Lorde's elapse of emotional stability, so she left the room in order to find Dade. Several minutes later, she discovered him inside of the waiting room for patients' families. When his head lifted from his knees due to her gentle touch on his back, she saw a man broken for the second time within a few minutes.

"Hey."

Dade didn't respond, instead, resting his head inside of SaeKu's chest as she kneeled before him. She paid no mind to the amount of pressure he was enforcing on her tender breast. Dade held onto her for what seemed as eternity, but was only a short period of time.

"Come on. Let's get you back in there."

Dade followed orders, following SaeKu back to Lorde's room. "He can't see." Dade managed to say just before they entered the room.

SaeKu halted movement, resting her head to the right side. Her mouth dropped, and she began to shake. "No. Don't say that." Her face contorted, crying was to follow. "Please. They've been through enough." SaeKu could bare no more bad news for the couple's sake. "Please."

Dade nodded, confirming what he'd just said. "I have to find out who did this to them. This is unacceptable. I need you to be aight with this shit, because some things are about to change. You hear?"

"Yes." SaeKu nodded.

"Good. First, I need you to go home." He demanded. "Get some rest, and I will let you know when to go get the girls. For now, I need you to rest up."

"Okay." SaeKu agreed. She was tired.

"Let's get your things, and I will walk you down."

Dade and SaeKu walked back inside of the room to find Lorde sleeping peacefully, again.

"SHIT." Dade mumbled, upset that he had neglected to get any answers from Lorde right away, knowing that he wouldn't have the strength to stay awake too long. Shrugging, he resolved to the fact that he had all the time in the world to wait this shit out. When Lorde woke, he'd be right there, again.

**

"Who did this to you?" Lorde heard as he searched for consciousness, again. "Tell me. Who did this?" Dade was over his bedside, wishing he would wake faster. He had noted him attempting from a far, and rushed over. "Just say the name." he demanded.

Fluttering a bit faster, the events of the terrible night replayed in Lorde's head. Forcing his eyes open, he searched for clarity within his sight. He'd prayed that when he woke, things would change, but nothing had given. Frustrated and confused, needing to blow off some steam, he tried speaking, but nothing would come from his mouth.

Dade noted dehydration, again, and poured him a cup of ice cold water that sat on the table beside the bed. After Lorde had gotten rid of the second cup, Dade was back in his face, waiting for answers. With a raised brow, he anticipated Lorde's answer.

"The doctor said that there is no explanation for my lost of vision. From the x-rays, the bullet missed this thin ass brain of mine. They don't understand. I don't understand. Man, how a nigga supposed to live like this?" Lorde knew that Dade wanted answers, but he wanted comfort. "To make matters worse, my girl in some damn institution clocked out from the world. I hear SaeKu crying more often than not when she swings through. Them niggas have got to get it."

"What niggas?" Dade listened intently, knowing that they were finally getting somewhere. "Sage handled the second person, but I was sure there was another."

"Jax and some fuck nigga... She really…" Lorde had no idea what had went down.

"Yeah."

"Well, that nigga Jax is the only one left."

"Say no more."

Dade slammed the cup on the table, and left Lorde to his sorrows. Dade was familiar with the name Jax, even more so because he had been trying to play boyfriend to his bitch. The fact that he'd gotten one up on his brother had Dade livid, burning from the inside out.

His feet moved hours behind his mind as he treaded through the hospital, one person in mind. Dade tore the highway up, disregarding stop lights and signs. By God's graces, he was peddling through the dimmed condo minutes later.

"Wake up!" based boomed through his vocals.

"Huh?" SaeKu was frightened by Dade's tone, afraid that he'd be the barrier of bad news once again. "What's wrong? Is everything alright?"

Searching for answers through the darkness, she was startled when the light came on. The brightness took some adjusting, causing SaeKu to scrunch her nose. She stared ahead at a visible disturbed Dade, wondering what the ruckus was about. His chest was swollen, and ear tips red like fire.

"No. Ain't shit aight!" Dade barked, pacing the floor. "I need a location on that nigga!"

"Dade, you have to be more clear. I don't understand." SaeKu was clueless.

"That fucking nigga you were calling yourself fucking with. I need a location on that bitch!" Venom flew from Dade's lips, burning SaeKu in the process. "That motherfucker did that shit to my peoples!" he pointed towards the door as if Lorde was standing on the other side of it. "Do you know what it must feel like to wake and not be able to see? Huh? The thought of me never seeing my girls again would eat me alive. Oh, and let's not mention his unborn child. Those sick motherfuckers murdered his unborn, and them bitches have to die."

"You're right." SaeKu agreed, nodding her head. "You're absolutely correct, Dade."

"You feel what I'm saying?" Dade was heated, chest lifting before falling with impact. SaeKu's head bobbed up and down, dramatically, not believing what she was hearing.

"Yes!" SaeKu replied. "Yes, baby. I can take you to him. I can tell you whatever you need to know." She was doing her best to comply, afraid to upset Dade any more than he was. For she partially felt responsible for the outcome of this situation, being that she was dating the man that had tormented their family.

"Na, I need you to go get my fucking kids and get ghost for a minute. Go home to Philly, and I'm coming for y'all when this shit blows over. I need to know everybody is safe. Them niggas ain't letting shit happen to y'all out there."

"Okay. Daicee, too?" SaeKu was curious.

"Daicee is one of mine, isn't she?" Dade snarled.

"Yes. I just… I didn't know if her mother would be okay with…"

"Right about now, fuck her mama. If I say she's rolling, then she's motherfucking rolling!"

"Okay Dade." SaeKu threw her hands in the air. "When should we be leaving?"

"Asap. But first, I need them digits and an address."

**

Dade was hunched down in the driver seat as he watched the home front intently. He'd gotten his family out of dodge hours prior, and didn't move a muscle until they were safe in the city that had birthed SaeKu. He'd called Alani and warned her that Daicee would be with him for a week or so. She had no objections, being that she had yet to heal from her injuries –completely.

Alone, not concerned with what the niggas from the block was willing to do for Lorde, he sought out the victim by his lonesome. See, Lorde's respect ran wide, and niggas were ready to lay their life on the line for him. However, it wasn't necessary. Besides, they were on some shoot first ask questions later, but Dade's mind was elsewhere. He needed to ask questions and shoot later. Moreover, this case was sensitive, unlike any other, which was the main reason he'd decided to ride the shit out solo.

Tap.

Tap.

Tap.

Dade upped his hammer, aiming it towards the window. Without as much as a questioning stare, he set his finger on the trigger and prepared to air that bitch out. A deep baritone halted his action, and caused a raised brow on his end.

Using his left hand to apply pressure to the window controller, he rolled it down before ducking his head. There were two tall, slender frames bent and staring back at him. A smirked crossed his handsome face, while pride pumped through his chest.

"We going on missions solo and shit, na?" Meek questioned with a shrug of the shoulders. "When you got a nigga that's been wondering how he could pay ya back for that good samaritan act you pulled way back when."

"And I'm just wondering why he figured laying on the couch sipping Coronas felt better than getting my hands wet? It's been a long time, yo."

"React first, think later. Caught between a rock and a hard place. My mans is down bad, and dumping on niggas was my first thought. Nothing. Nobody. Only blood. Lots of it." Dade admitted. "Jump in. Don't blow up the spot." He hit the locks, and both men jumped in. "How did..."

"SaeKu wanted to make sure that her man made it back to her. Thank God for that, or we wouldn't have known shit."

Nodding, Dade mentally thanked his baby girl for looking out for his well-being. Before he could speak again, a black Altima pulled into the driveway that he had been keeping an eye out for.

"Action!" he bounced up and down in his seat, adrenaline pumping just as much as it had been when the tap pursued his attention.

The car doors swung open, swiftly, each man pulling their hoodies snug around their faces. The dark of the night shielded RahMeek, but Roc and Dade's faces were catching the street lights as they passed. Quiet, like thieves in the night, they crept up on the unsuspecting victim. Dade pointed forward, getting a clear understanding of the direction that he was taking. Roc nodded to the left, and RahMeek headed to the right. Each man walked at a swift and steady pace, neither ahead of the other.

Dade's adrenaline pumped as he made contact with the highly paved side walk. Lifting his leg, he was sure not to miss the step and fuck up the entire plan. As he dissected the situation, he realized his victim was alone.

Perfect. Dade thought. He wasn't in the mood for killing innocent people.

No one accompanied him as he removed himself from the vehicle after shutting it off. He continued to spit the rhymes of one of Ice Cube's hit tracks as he bobbed his head, unaware of the danger that lurked in the shadows. Dade wanted to dump on that nigga on site, but he had some shit to prove. Dade needed his prey to know and understand that the one thing you didn't fuck with was a Livingston. Lorde, Sage, SaeKu, Dido, Daicee, and Pryce were off limits, and anyone that fucked with them had to see him. It was a no-brainer.

Just as the victim reached his walkway, Dade snuck up on him.

Prrrrrrrrrrrrrrr.

He whistled, causing him to look behind him –

surveying his surroundings. Dade chuckled at the irony of the

situation. "Little too late to be scoping. We here, now,

nigga." Both Roc and Meek appeared on either side,

surrounding him with their arms folded in front of them.

Dade, on the other hand had taken the silencer from his back

pocket and started screwing it onto the mouth of his pistol as

he spoke.

"Lorde Livingston. Sage King. Unborn child, shit we

hadn't even named." Dade tried to blow off some steam

before making his next move, but he was hot. Furious. "Jax,

it is?" he questioned, finally looking at the man's life that he

was about to end.

A brown paper bag full of paper for rolling, a Colt 45,

and some loose cigs fell to the ground as he looked into

Dade's envious glare. The gleam of the Rolex watch that

hugged Jax's wrist caught Dade by surprise.

He and Lorde had copped matching Rollies some

time ago. It angered Dade even more to know that this nigga

was a petty thief, along with being a rapist and wana-be

killer. "I take that as a yes." Dade shrugged. Lifting his right arm, he aimed at Jax's upper body. That blood that he'd been imagining was closer than ever, now.

"Jax, boy. You ready to meet your maker, nigga?" Dade asked before fire erupted from his gun.

Chapter Fourteen

Doctor's didn't have a medical explanation for the lost of eyesight on Lorde's behalf. Their only conclusion was that the injuries he'd sustained had caused a delay, and his brain wasn't sending the signals it needed to contribute to functioning eye sight. Whatever the case was, Lorde was dealing with it. He used his fingers to locate the hate that Dade had brought to prepare for his home going. He'd been inside of the hospital for over a month, and was ready to blow the joint.

"You ready?" he asked Dade.

"Yeah. I'm good."

"Let's roll. We have one stop to make." He warned.

"Come on, man. You know what I'm trying to do!" Lorde had one thing on his mind, and that was making it home.

"I know. The quicker you move, nigga, the sooner we will get there." Dade stood behind Lorde and guided him through the hospital. He refused to be handicapped with a wheelchair or a cane –so guidance would have to suffice.

Dade got Lorde squared away in the car before pulling off and heading to their first destination. After cutting off onto a dirt rode, Dade rode for three miles before coming to a halt. Lorde had lost his sight, but his memory was still in tact.

He tried his hardest to adjust to the blurriness, but to no avail. The condition was frustrating to say the least, but he was happy to be alive. He wanted to be certain that they were in the place that he had frequented.

"Dade." He called out for confirmation, frustrated that he couldn't see.

"Yes." Dade confirmed.

"You…" Lorde started.

"Yeah. I couldn't take that from you man." Dade admitted.

He'd wounded Jax, but let the nigga breathe. He wouldn't take the opportunity away from his brother, although it had permitted itself. Dade knew how much that would mean to Lorde, so they packed that nigga up and brought him to the chop shop.

"If I ain't never told you this shit… I fucking love you man!" Lorde's voice cracked. He was on the brink of tears, but held back. He felt so weak and vulnerable with his eye sight being snatched from him. Everything was so much more effective.

"I love you, too, yo! You gone be aight. You hear me?" Lorde reached over and squeezed Lorde's hand. "As long as I got breath in my fucking body, then you good nigga. I'm all the motherfucking eyes you need to see! Alright. Don't let this shit defeat you! We better than that. Momma raised up to man up, not step down. We in this shit."

"You right man. Let me go handle this shit so that I can get home to my people."

Lorde hung close by Dade, counting on him to lead him to his victim. He was in no mode to stay and fuck around. He simply wanted to end this nigga, and get back to his girl and daughter. Sage's condition had been heavy on his mind, and felt like he was the missing piece to her puzzle. He knew that once she saw he was okay, she'd be good. He'd insisted that they bring her home from that damn institution, because it wasn't shit they could do for her that her family couldn't.

"Here." Lorde felt Dade stuff a chrome plated pistol in his hand. "Aim straight ahead and you can't miss."

Lorde nodded, tuning in to the sounds around him. It was no myth, when one of your senses were null, the other's were heightened. Lorde listened for movement, and found it the minute Jax attempted to lift his head. He was so weak and skinny that it didn't make since.

He was surviving from bread and water that Dade decided to feed him whenever he felt like stopping by. He was only keeping him alive so that Lorde could kill him. Jax was only a fixture of the man that he used to be. His skin was pale, hair was a mess, face was unrecognizable, and body was slim.

Lifting the gun that he'd been giving, Lorde aimed in the direction that the sound had come from. He heard the effects of the first bullet as Jaz fell backwards in the chair. Dade stared on in complete silence, shocked beyond belief. There was no way in hell that a blind man should be able to aim so fucking precisely, and hit it's target with one shot.

Lorde, then, fired again and again. Dade reached out and tapped his shoulder to cease the fire. "He's out of here. You hit him on the first shot."

Jax laid on the concrete floor with his head leaking. Lorde was a cold motherfucker, and Dade would have to give him his props.

"Let's get out of here." Dade grabbed the gun, and placed it on safety. After stuffing it inside of his pocket, he led Lorde back out to the car. Lorde sat in silence as they journeyed to Dade's condo. It was where everyone was cooped up at for the time being.

Dade guided Lorde into the house, and he was instantly swarmed by Daicee and Pryce. Bending down, Lorde pulled Pryce into his arms. He'd missed his little one.

"Me miss you, daddy!" Pryec spoke, hugging Lorde's neck.

"I missed you, too. Where's mommy?"

"Her there." She pointed to the room that SaeKu had prepared for Sage and Lorde.

"Okay. Daddy will be right back."

Lorde put Pryce down, but she wasn't far behind him. She followed him into the room that Dade had helped him find. When they walked inside, Sage was standing by the window, as usual. She didn't bother to turn her head, not even when the children began to cause a ruckus.

Lorde heard her shift, placing her weight on her other side. She'd been standing for some time now. His heart pounded out of his chest. It felt so good to be in her presence, again –even after everything that had gone down.

"Sage," he called out to her.

Swiftly, her neck turned, head facing in his direction. Dade wanted to run out of the room screaming. They'd tried everything just to get her to even look their way, but got nothing. Now that Lorde was in her presence, she was coming around.

"Lorde." She spoke lowly at first, but then said it louder. "Lorde! You're here. You're alive. You're … I…" no more words were exchanged. Instead, Sage rushed to him and wrapped her arms around his body. "I love you!" she panted, eyes full of tears. "I love you!" she repeated over and over.

"I love you, too. It's okay. We're both okay."

"We're okay." She nodded, not wanting to let go of her man.

"Yeah." Lorde thought about the fact that he had been shortened of his vision.

A tear slipped from Lorde's eye, followed by a stream of others. He was happy to be in the company of his family, but it tore him to pieces not to be able to see his baby girl's face, and Sage's either. Dade recognized the pain that was written in his expression.

"I need to lay down." Exhaustion wore him down.

He was emotionally drained more than anything. He pulled away from Sage, and kissed her cheek. Dade helped him to the bed, and Sage followed close behind. Dade left them to their lonesome and took the children with him. Just like that, Sage had snapped out of whatever trance the robbery and rape had placed her end.

After getting settled in, Lorde called out to Sage. Pulling her down to the bed with him, he pulled her in closer to his chest. He'd missed that more than anything. While they both laid silently, listening to one another's breathing, Lorde tried to find the words to reveal his condition, but was immediately consumed with emotion.

There hadn't been a time that Lorde could remember hurting from the inside out. Even when his mother had passed, he couldn't remember shedding a tear. Motor mouth, loud, boisterous, and macho all of his life, Lorde felt minute all of a sudden –small, nonexistent, handicapped, and crippled. Saddened by his circumstances, the words to express himself transformed into tears. One by one, they slid down his cheeks and onto the white linen on the bed. He'd given Sage enough grief. Anything more would bring her world crumbling down. Holding the love of his life as if he would never see her again, Lorde closed his eyes and allowed sleep to overcome him.

... The End

Thanks for reading. Hope that you enjoyed.

Made in the USA
Columbia, SC
24 May 2017